IN THE CHINESE MOUNTAINS

JOHN HOPKINS

In the Chinese Mountains

A NOVEL OF PERU

PETER OWEN · LONDON

PETER OWEN PUBLISHERS
73 Kenway Road London SW5 0RE

First published in Great Britain 1990
© John Hopkins 1990

ISBN 0–7206–0803–1

Typeset by Selectmove London
Printed in Great Britain by Billings of Worcester

For Ellen Ann, Jonathan, Beau and Cabell

PART

I

Nobody, not even her grandfather Charlie whom she adored, was ever able to exert much authority over my cousin Rosalinda. She insisted on wearing trousers and bobbed her black hair 'to look like an Indian'. The furnishings of her room consisted of a bed, a desk and an old truck tyre that she had come upon during her ceaseless ramblings around Arequipa. She had rolled it home and had managed, with the aid of some team-mates secretly summoned during the siesta hour, to carry it upstairs. She would heave it from one corner of her room to the other, stand on it and admire the photographs of the famous soccer stars she had tacked to the walls. As her bedroom was located directly above the sitting room, the family knew by the rumbling above their heads that Rosalinda was gazing at the stars instead of doing her homework. She was then about fourteen years old.

She would also position the tyre beneath the window, climb up on it, and stare for hours at the high white wall of the Santa Catalina convent across the street. Her practice of writing notes, of making gliders of them, and of hurling them out of the window so they sailed over the convent wall, earned Charlie a visit from Archbishop Nineth de Cisneros.

Nothing could have been more innocent than the contents of these notes which, when the Archbishop had departed, made Charlie roar with laughter. They all began with the same lengthy greeting:

Whoever you are, whoever finds this letter, I know that you have journeyed hundreds of miles over the dusty roads of this bone-strewn land, that you have joyously walked barefoot wearing nothing but leaves and branches to cover yourselves, only to wait for years in the streets in order to be admitted to Santa Catalina, to become the brides of Jesus, never to be seen again in the world. Why? Whoever you are (you are so close that I imagine I can hear you breathing on the other side of the wall), I wish to know you. If I cannot know you, please know me.

What followed (the Archbishop had arrived with a sheaf of these letters, gathered, he claimed, from the roofs and gutters of the convent) might be an account of her day's activities or a naïve question concerning the existence of God. More often than not they contained detailed descriptions of what she had seen while roaming around Arequipa (usually to and from a soccer match): the deplorable conditions in the *barriadas*, or shantytowns, that ringed the city; the growing numbers of the homeless; the desperation of the children; the sparse attendance in churches.

One essay, entitled *Christmas Spirit*, was a typical example:

Fights constantly break out among the ambulatory vendors who choke Bolivar and the other main shopping streets, as they jostle for elbow room at the most lucrative positions. They scratch and bite and use the most filthy language, especially the women. My mother and I were pushed and shoved all along the street. The police vans arrived right before our eyes. The soldiers jumped out and started to kick and punch everyone in sight, which included not a few innocent Christmas shoppers. We took refuge in a doorway with a vendor of plastic toys who took no notice of what was happening in the street. He just emptied his pockets and hummed contentedly to himself as he counted the few pennies he had earned between raids. Meanwhile, women were running around screaming, with blood streaming down their faces. All they wanted was to sell the few trinkets they'd made themselves at home, so they could buy Christmas presents for their own children and families. As soon as the soldiers retired, the vendors assembled as before, as crowds will happily fill the streets after rain. There was a sense of shared relief as people laughed and wiped away the blood. The newspapers are full of it, but nothing can be done. The officials are confounded, and the police are harassed. There are just too many desperate souls to contend with, surging down from the shantytowns with their cheap goods.

Although it was never known whether these airborne epistles ever fell into the hands of anyone other than the Mother Superior, Rosalinda's window was locked, and notes ceased to fly over the convent wall.

Her great passion was soccer. She spent her afternoons once school was out kicking a ball over the dusty vacant lots on the outskirts of Arequipa, where she captained a team made up of herself and ten Indian boys from the shantytowns. The games, contested by young people already accustomed to fighting for their lives, regularly erupted in brawls; and Rosalinda often returned home covered with cuts and bruises. Her family was horrified. Nevertheless, she prevailed upon Charlie to furnish uniforms for her team, known as 'Strongest' – a name taken from the motto on the truck tyre. The tyre was rolled to every game, and the team went on to win an urban championship. An account of the final match was written up in the newspaper. Rosalinda was described as 'that mysterious and dark-haired beauty and Strongest's swiftest player, who headed in one goal, assisted Eduardito with two others, and led ten young men, resplendent in crimson, to victory and, who can say, perhaps even a future.' The ardent reporter, who had somehow discovered the connection with Charlie, went on to proclaim that Rosalinda, 'whose forebear is one of the most successful presidents that Peru has produced this century, has provided an example which is both glittering and poignant, and one to which our more wealthy and aristocratic families would do well to pay attention.'

That was the last straw. Shortly after that, Rosalinda was packed off to boarding school in England.

2

While she was away, I arrived from Santa Cruz, in Bolivia, to enter the University of San Agustín in Arequipa. Naturally, the first thing I did was to telephone my cousins. I was invited to Sunday lunch in their grand colonial townhouse in Cathedral Square, where my uncle, Joshua Calderón, welcomed me like a long-lost son. Rosalinda's father was a stocky, gentle man in his mid-forties. Bald, with a round face, bushy eyebrows and deep-set eyes, he had a shy smile and a serene manner. A farmer and family man, he exuded warmth and sensitivity. His children were continually running up and throwing their arms around him.

Aunt Mary was by contrast tall, thin and reserved. Her eyes glittered with the weary expression of an Englishwoman who has raised seven children in Peru. Those eyes never stopped scrutinizing my face, my scars, and my skin.

Rosalinda's little brothers and sisters had dressed up as cowboys and Indians to greet me. Probably they had expected me to arrive wearing feathers. With them pulling on my fingers and clothes, I was propelled into the sitting room and was introduced to Charlie, who occupied a chair by the window.

'Charlie, this is James, George's son, from Santa Cruz,' Uncle Joshua said. 'He's going to study engineering at the university.'

Charlie was a leathery, desiccated octogenarian with a shock of straight white hair. He reminded me of a chameleon whose attention has been attracted by a fly, as he slowly rotated his gaze and riveted me with a long, cold look.

'The United States is the world's most powerful nation,' he rasped, 'and the Panama Canal is the greatest engineering wonder of the world. In Panama, I came upon a thirsty tiger in a zoo, and made sure it was given water. And elephants, sonny, must have salt. *Salt!*'

The children screamed with laughter. 'It's an act,' Uncle Joshua whispered. 'Last week he took the children to the circus to see the elephant, and there was no elephant. Charlie raised such a storm that the authorities, to palliate his anger, closed the circus. He's in a bad mood because Rosalinda's not here. Ever since she left he's been pretending to be crazy so we'll bring her back from England.'

Charlie Calderón – also known as 'The Cork' for his ability to stay afloat in politically troubled waters – had been President of Peru for two, but not successive, terms of office. He had fought a successful war with Ecuador, enlarged the frontiers of the republic, raised the price of guano, and confounded his political enemies. The country had actually united behind him. Less publicized were his cruel reprisals against the Indians, for which he was still hated.

When he retired from politics, he was content never to do another stroke of work. He turned down a lucrative offer from a publishing house in Buenos Aires to bring out his memoirs. The weight of his silence, combined with advanced age, gave his unsolicited pronouncements an eerie, prophetic ring. Nobody dared challenge him; everybody but Rosalinda was scared of him. He gardened a little; his one great pleasure was to take Rosalinda fishing.

What with the roast beef, Yorkshire pudding and all the trimmings, Sunday lunch was a very English affair. Aunt Mary insisted on it. The children were encouraged to speak English at table. It was an amiable feast and a special event in the life of the Calderón family. Sunday was the one day in the week that Uncle Joshua was there. The rest of the week he spent on his farm, arriving home Saturday night and departing again Monday. So for Sunday lunch the close-knit family was at last together. A breathless, almost passionate exchange of information – news about the farm, adventures in school, bits of gossip and politics – flowed back and forth across the table. I sat there fascinated, and at the same time trying to fight off a feeling of resentment and jealousy towards my happy, well-to-do, white-skinned cousins. It was hard for me not to feel these things.

Unlike most of the old-established families of Peru, the Calderóns had never been the absentee landlords of various farms and ranches scattered about the country; nor were they the owners of mines. The family had traditionally served the State and over the years had provided it with some distinguished diplomats and ministers; most recently with Charlie the Great. The Calderóns' principal asset was Juanpablo farm, which had been in the family since the time of the Conquest. It wasn't a big farm as farms in Peru go, a thousand acres more or less, located about a four-hour drive from Arequipa.

Charlie had rarely set foot in the place because he was too busy pursuing his political career, but he had sent his children there for the holidays. My father never stopped talking about it; all his fondest childhood memories came from Juanpablo. When Uncle Joshua came home from Harvard, he found the farm fallen into dismal neglect. It produced hardly enough food to feed the Indians who worked it. Cotton was the main crop then.

'You need slave labour to make a cash crop out of cotton these days,' he told me. 'Unfortunately, a lot of farms in Peru are still being run that way.'

He ploughed up the cotton and planted fruit trees. While the trees were maturing, he cultivated vegetables and raised chickens. Every day a load of tomatoes, melons, potatoes, coriander, eggs and so forth used to go by truck to the market in Arequipa to be sold. With their own hands Uncle Joshua and the Indians built a dam to ensure that there would always be an adequate supply of water to irrigate the crops when the river ran dry, which it did each summer. A miniature hydroelectric plant was installed to bring electricity to the farm. He planted vines and in a few years began to bottle his own *pisco*. The trees at last started to bear fruit. Now each Granny Smith and Golden Delicious was wrapped in tissue paper by the same pair of Indian hands that had picked it. By truck they came to Arequipa, then by Fawcett Airlines to Lima, where they were airfreighted directly to Europe and the US. Uncle Joshua's apples and plums were consumed in New York and Montreal. His cherries could be found in São Paulo, and his strawberries went all the way to Stockholm for Christmas.

During lunch he read aloud a letter from Rosalinda, who had discovered his pears, individually packed in the distinctive Juanpablo wrappings she herself had designed, at Harrods.

> To the amazement of everyone around me, I ecstatically devoured several of them on the spot and presented the cashier with the cores. I left the store happy and full and at the same time feeling hollow inside and close to tears.

Throughout the meal Charlie sat silent and inscrutable; he just stared out the window at El Misti. I, too, felt mesmerized by the sight of the monstrous snow dome that blocked out half the sky. Nineteen thousand feet high, the volcano presided over Arequipa like a sinister brooding giant.

Charlie, noticing my gaze, gave a sly grin and rasped, 'Back in '68 the ground shook so hard that horses broke their legs standing up.'

'He's talking about 1868, when the city was completely wrecked by an earthquake,' Uncle Joshua explained.

Aunt Mary crossed herself during the ensuing silence. Everyone in Arequipa unconsciously awaited the day when El Misti must inevitably stir once more from its timeless sleep and trigger another earthquake. In the Calderón house, all the beds were set inside deep niches in the massive stone walls. In an earthquake the roofs of most buildings collapsed, but the walls, if they were thick enough, could endure the shock, and the sleeper had a chance of surviving.

After lunch the children got me out in the garden and bombarded me with questions. Could I tame the deadly fer-de-lance by catching it by the tail and whirling it about my head until it was dizzy? Who would win in a battle – the anaconda or the jaguar? Was it true that jungle Indians steal little children to boil them down and turn them into buckets of paste? How many minutes did it take a school of piranhas to devour a live pig? And so forth.

They showed me a cottage out back that Aunt Mary had transformed into a private chapel. A renegade priest arrived every other week to say a secret, illegal Latin mass. Aunt Mary, I was also told, harboured a morbid fear of lizards. The day before, the children had found a gecko that she had stomped on in her rose garden. They nailed it to a tiny cross and laid it on the altar to see if God would bring it back to life.

'I used to eat lizards,' I told them.

3

At my first-term break Uncle Joshua invited me to the farm. On the way I had to answer a hundred friendly questions about my father, his older brother, whom he had not seen in many years. George Calderón had emigrated to Santa Cruz, Bolivia, right after he had finished Harvard. That was more than twenty years ago. In those days Santa Cruz was hailed as the frontier of the future, the land of opportunity where you could raise three crops of corn a year. Virgin forests were there for the cutting, and oil strikes were making the headlines. The Government was virtually giving the land away to attract settlers to a remote jungle region where 'women outnumber men eight to one, the prettiest girls in Bolivia.'

Fortunately for him, my father married a distant cousin, a sensible Arequipeña, before setting out; otherwise he probably would have made an even worse mess of his life than he did.

Those were the days when the local machos swaggered along the streets of Santa Cruz with six-guns strapped to their hips. The potholes on Main Street were so deep that jeeps got stuck and had to be extracted by teams of mules. My father first tried his hand at the lumber business. He soon learned that he had to cut down as many as 500 trees to get to the one mahogany. When his heavy machinery, imported at vast expense from the US, sank out of sight in the swamp, he bought land and planted rice. After five years of drought, he went off to Rio on a secret mission. The Bolivian Government later decorated him for smuggling a bag full of pepper plants out of Brazil. The seedlings thrived, but my father, either from lack of funds or foresight, supported the climbing pepper plants with wooden posts instead of metal stakes. At harvest time, when he should have been on the road to riches, the posts were attacked by termites and collapsed. The entire crop was lost. My mother and father were reduced to panning for gold in the wilderness of Beni Province.

It was there, at the confluence of the Mamoré and Tijamuchi rivers in the middle of the jungle, that I came into the picture. After a last futile effort to filter gold flakes from a sandbar, my parents were about to set off in their canoe when an Indian woman stepped from the forest, leading a blond child by the hand. That was me.

The woman explained that my father was a German missionary, long since departed. I was then eight years old. Because of my extreme ugliness – meaning my Indian features, blond hair and rough, yellowish skin – I was treated as a scapegoat by our tribe. My face beneath one eye had been burned repeatedly with hot irons, causing me to squint and the eye to run permanently. Due to famine in the village, my Indian mother feared that I would be tortured again, perhaps killed. She implored my parents to take me away with them.

My mother and father held a short, emotional debate by the river. My mother, childless in ten years of marriage, prevailed. I stepped into their canoe, waved goodbye to my Indian mother, and paddled away to a new life.

My father got a Toyota dealership and settled down. I was sent to school, where I learned Spanish and English. My tear ducts were repaired by surgery. My eye no longer weeps, but the scars remain and so, unfortunately, does the twisted expression. At school I would have stayed an outcast had I not been able to run faster and jump farther than my fellows. They experimented with bows and arrows; given a blow pipe I could have brought down a monkey or parrot from a tree. My parents gave me their affection but never really knew what to do with me. I couldn't blame them for that: a half-breed has no place in Spanish society. My adoptive grandfather may have been President of Peru, but I felt more at home among the shoeshine boys and petty criminals who worked and slept on Main Street. They, like me, were struggling to leave behind their poverty-stricken Indian past and come to terms with a world that did not want them. The sleepy little town of

Santa Cruz, I might add, has become the cocaine capital of the world. There's an international airport, and my friends, who were shining shoes a few years ago, now go about with satchels full of thousands of American dollars with a loaded revolver sitting on top. So much money changes hands that Main Street is now called 'Wall Street'. The guns are still there and so are the potholes. The brand new Range Rovers and Super Toyotas with huge tyres and tinted glass have to be winched to safety right there in front of the church.

My father, alarmed by the company I was keeping, resolved to send me away to school. He wanted me to go to Harvard but didn't have the money. The University of San Agustín in Arequipa was the next best thing.

4

We spotted Juanpablo miles away – a ribbon of green between two arid hills. Everything else as far as the eye could see was desert. Grey dunes had formed on the orange plain. I could taste the pumice between my teeth – ancient fallout from El Misti.

Uncle Joshua, who had been driving fast over the dusty roads, eased up on the accelerator. Relaxing after the long drive, he smiled at the sight of the farm ahead.

'You know, James, all my life I've wanted to be a farmer,' he said. 'Growing up in the Presidential Palace in Lima, I'd had my fill of politics by the time I was twenty. For me, Juanpablo represented reality. When I told Charlie that I wanted to be a farmer, all he said was, "Farming is dull, son. Farm communities are dull", and went back to his papers. You know, it gave me a bit of a complex.'

Was it this declaration, I wondered, that prompted Charlie to hand over Juanpablo to 'dull' Uncle Joshua, as he was known in my family, when it should rightfully have gone to my father? It wasn't until years later, when he was broke and not even the invocation of Charlie's name could extract another penny from the bank, that he regretted not staying home and demanding his inheritance. Embittered by failure, he had never returned to Arequipa.

Uncle Joshua smiled and happily acknowledged the Indians' salutes as we sped up to the farm. Ahead stood a pair of huge pine trees that dated from the time when men wore armour. The whitewashed arches of the hacienda reflected the afternoon sun. After so much desolation, it was like arriving in an oasis.

After lunch and a siesta, I put on my boots and went for a walk up the valley. I wandered through orchards of apple, pear, plum, peach and pomegranate. Everywhere was the sound of running water. The Indian farmers had brought the irrigation canals, which originated at the dam miles up the valley, down to their little plots of coriander and onions. Doves and falcons and other strange birds flitted about in the hour before sunset. The mud huts of the Indians stood half hidden among the poplars. I was greeted cheerily whenever I looked down upon the terraced plots where the Indian women sang and with sickles harvested the grass that they would feed their animals. The children shouted and ran about making bundles. Everything was lush and green. When the breeze moved the poplars, they showed the silvery backs of their leaves.

With the sun sinking behind a ridge, I crossed a dusty soccer pitch where Indian boys were kicking a ball. At the end of the pitch I stopped and looked up the narrow valley to where the orchards extended to meet the base of the eroded mountain. Here was order, productivity and peace. Juanpablo was undoubtedly the model for the farm that my father had always dreamed of creating: a farm that would have provided his family with food; a farm where his children would have learned about seasons and regeneration; a farm that would have paid for their education at the best schools; a farm that would have been a spiritual haven to which they would always return. What he got was a Toyota dealership and me. A place like this would never be his, or mine, unless something happened – God forbid – to Uncle Joshua and all his children.

The moaning wind began to stir dust eddies on the pitch. The temperature dropped, and I turned back towards the house. From one side of the pitch the wind carried voices. I went over and looked down into a hollow. Uncle Joshua was squatting on his haunches in the dust, surrounded by Indians. Speaking in their own language, they were asking questions which he was trying to answer. Soon it became so dark that all that remained visible was Uncle Joshua's white shirt, the shapes of the Indians squatting around him, and the glow of their cigarettes. It was a strangely intimate scene, and I didn't want to interfere. As I went away, the wind carried the same insistent enquiries, Uncle Joshua's measured replies, and the sound of the Indians coughing and spitting.

That evening, while he mixed up the *pisco* sours, I told him what I had seen.

'Every week we talk like that.' He poured out the foaming drinks. 'We start off with the farm and move on to politics – always politics.'

'What do they want to know?'

'What's going on in the world. They're like peasants everywhere – nobody tells them anything. So I tell them – the good and the bad, the attempts at land reform and the trouble up in the Sierra. What the Government is doing or trying to do. I look forward to our talks and so do they. I owe you an apology. This afternoon I was driving too fast, but I was afraid I would be late for them.'

Uncle Joshua's face was lit by the same paternal glow as when his children ran up to embrace him, or when the Indians waved from the fields. He enjoyed being a father to them all.

'We always return to the eternal preoccupation – that is, when is land reform going to come? What they mean is – when am I going to turn this farm over to them? They all know that Juanpablo has belonged to our family since the Conquest, but they ask, before that who did it belong to? I say, before that it was a desert. But we all know . . . before that . . . everything, even the desert, was theirs.'

We carried our drinks on to the veranda and looked out over the valley.

'Five years ago, during the Peasant Revolution, truckloads of Indians arrived from the shantytowns to occupy this farm. I was driven out and thought I'd never see this valley again. Then the tales came – how they'd slaughtered the chickens and the livestock and eaten the fruit before it was ripe. Within six months they were starving, and vegetables had to be brought from the market in Arequipa to feed them. I went to church and begged God not to let me rejoice in the misfortune of others.'

The memory caused an uncharacteristic ripple of pain to furrow Uncle Joshua's brow.

22

'When it was all over and the junta gave this farm back, it took me three years to get Juanpablo back to where it was before. I built a school, and there's a resident teacher. Now we have a clinic and a trained nurse. A doctor comes twice a year to give injections. We have a church, and a priest visits once a month to say mass. At Rosalinda's insistence, there's a soccer pitch. And the wages have gone up and up and up. They're a lot better off and they know it, but they still go on asking the same question. They think that if they keep on asking often enough and long enough, they will get what they want – like prayer.' He sipped his drink thoughtfully. 'Maybe they will in the end. In their quiet way they are waiting for us to leave. They have patiently borne a grudge that is 400 years old, and I understand it. The year of my exile I went to church every day to rid myself of hate. And do you know what the priest said? "Be patient, my son, and Juanpablo will be restored to you." Our visiting priest here – I think he's a bit of a red – probably tells our Indians the same thing. I can tolerate the idea of *them* having Juanpablo one day, but the rabble from the shantytowns . . . never.'

'Uncle Joshua, you understand the Indians, you have their confidence, and you speak their language. At the next election, you should run for President. With the Indians behind you, you could turn all of Peru into a garden, just like it once was – self-sufficient and rich, and needing nothing from the rest of the world.'

Uncle Joshua's laugh was a little clicking sound. There was a twinkle in his deep-set eyes as he patted me on the back. Then his expression grew more serious.

'As a matter of fact, Charlie's old political party the CDU has been putting out feelers for me to be their candidate in the next election – if there ever is one. I keep telling them that I have no stomach for politics, that I am a farmer. I have no knowledge of anything but farming. The year of my exile I felt trapped in the city. I was completely at loose ends and had what I guess you would call a nervous breakdown. . . .'

This admission frightened me. Uncle Joshua, who was so sane, so sober, and so composed . . . his family and many others depended upon him. The idea of the rock crumbling was almost unimaginable.

'No, I am sure that I would make a very bad president,' he concluded. 'Too soft-hearted and too liberal. "Infected" by doubt and guilt. Mary criticized me for doing nothing to get the farm back, but I was paralysed by the truth.'

'What truth?'

'That the farm does not belong to me.'

'Then you think it belongs to. . . ?'

'The Indians.'

I was a little disappointed when he said that. What I was hoping he would say was that Juanpablo, or at least half of it, belonged to my father and me. 'Uh, is that what you really think?' I asked.

'Let me put it this way – my long association with the Indians has made me appreciate their point of view and doubt my own. Doubt would not be a virtue for the leader of the nation. Guilt held me back, and might do so again.'

'But in your heart do you really believe that Juanpablo should be handed over to the Indians?'

'Not just Juanpablo – all of Peru.'

I was astounded. 'Uncle Joshua, if you made that pledge in an election campaign every Indian in Peru would vote for you, not just once but over and over again, and you would be President for life.'

'Yes, but to make such a pledge would be political suicide. The idea is far too radical for any political party to swallow. No one, not even the Communists, would have me. And of course the army would never let me take office. I agree that the implications are almost unthinkable, but sometimes you have to think the unthinkable to ward off a catastrophe.'

'But could it really be made to work?'

He nodded gravely. 'It's the only long-term solution. It'll take many years, but one has to start sometime, because sooner or later, just as El Misti must one day erupt, the Indians are going to take back Peru. There are just too many of them, and too few of us. Of course, you can't turn back the clock – 450 years of history cannot be erased. But Peru is Indian as much as South Africa is black.' He stared out into the darkness. 'One day the power must be given to the people, or they'll take it by violence. There'll be a civil war that will rip Peru apart. Do you realize that in some inaccessible regions, the Indians still dress in animal skins and live in virtual Stone Age conditions? They're the true Peruvians – illiterate, half-starved, speaking only the Quechua tongue. There are millions of them – and they are waiting to take their country back.'

'Would it mean that everyone of Spanish descent would have to leave?' I tried to visualize such an exodus. It seemed inconceivable.

'I don't think so, but we would have to live as equals in a truly democratic society, without hoarding the power, the wealth and the land for ourselves.'

'Can a Harvard graduate live on equal terms with an illiterate Indian?'

'I've been living with them for years. Most of the decisions that affect the running of this farm are made jointly, at that little powwow you just witnessed. We have to start somewhere, James. Why not now? It'll be the end of Peru unless something is done quickly. But, if I run for President, I'll have to run as a farmer, and keep these thoughts to myself. I hope you can keep everything that I've told you a secret, because only two people – you and Rosalinda – know the vision of Peru that I hold in my heart.'

'Doesn't Charlie know?'

'Charlie?' Uncle Joshua chuckled. 'Charlie's an old-fashioned conquistador and Indian fighter. In his heart of hearts he hates the Indians. Yes, it's the sad truth. He looks upon them as inferiors, no better than serfs. Talk like this would be blasphemy to his ears. He'd brand me public enemy number one, and maybe even reach for his pistol.'

'He wouldn't kill his own son?' I asked, horrified.

'He's done worse things.'

'What things?'

'It's better not to talk about them.'

'I'm a member of the family, an adopted one, but a member nevertheless.'

'Well, if you must know,' he began reluctantly, 'when the Indian miners staged that one-day sitdown at Cerro de Pasco during his first term of office, there was no need to send in the army, but he did. It started out as a peaceful demonstration against unsafe working conditions, but it turned into mass murder. They said that 200 miners died when an earth tremor caused the Gordo mineshaft to collapse.' He looked grim. 'The true figure was closer to a thousand – men, women and children herded at gunpoint down the mine – and the tremor was caused by dynamite detonated on Charlie's orders. The miners and their families were buried alive.'

'Why would he do such a thing?'

'Because he'd heard there were Communists involved in the strike.'

'Were there?'

'Maybe there were, but no one lived to tell the tale. Then there was that other time when a group of dispossessed Indians squatted on some land that didn't belong to them. You know, one of those huge *latifundios* near Huanta where you see a sheep every ten miles. It was owned by one of our wealthy families who had never set foot on it in their lives. Anyway, the Indians knocked down a fence and put up their pitiful dwellings. The owners – I won't mention any names – rang up Charlie and demanded action. He sent in the army again and the whole lot were mowed down. No one knows how many were killed because there weren't any survivors. The bulldozers came, and they were all shoved into a mass grave.'

I thought of Charlie, surrounded by his grandchildren. 'What made him do such barbaric things?'

'Impatience and intolerance. To make a problem go away and because he has no respect for the Indians.'

'Does Rosalinda know this?'

'No – God, no!' Uncle Joshua almost shouted. 'And don't you ever tell her!'

'I promise not to, but won't she find out in the end?'

'I'll tell her one day . . . after Charlie's dead.' He looked glumly over the valley. 'In an unjust society the skeletons keep piling up in the closet . . . until one day the closet can't hold any more, and the door just bursts open.'

Smoke from the Indian huts spiralled through the trees into the clear, still night. It was hard to believe that in such a tranquil setting a bloody revolution could be smouldering.

5

During the next three years, while I was a student at the university, I learned about the instability of the earth, the instability of government, and the instability of my own soul. Arequipa was periodically rocked by seismic tremors. Few did much damage, and most went unnoticed by the general public. One morning a stone dislodged from the cathedral tower killed a leftist priest passing in the street. Aunt Mary, upon learning of the incident, claimed that she had stomped a lizard in her garden at precisely the same instant. The churches and houses in the city centre dated from colonial times and were built to withstand such shocks; it was in the *barriadas* where the damage was done. The carnage was duly described in the newspapers:

> The shantytown dwellers were reported to be sleeping at the time (5.30 a.m.), and the few witnesses said they first saw sheets of aluminium and zinc fly over. Then the factory wall – 100 yards long and 45 feet high – collapsed on to 27 'precarious' dwellings, burying people under tons of rubble, killing 17.
>
> 'Get me out of here, I can't stand it any longer', was the cry heard for hours from under the debris. Some of the victims were brought out mutilated and unrecognizable, while several children appeared unhurt after being trapped for hours.

We also listened to the distant rumblings from Lima, where junta replaced junta. The colonels borrowed so much money to equip the army that half the country's hard currency earnings went to service the foreign debt. They nationalized everything – agriculture, the fishmeal industry – and created a monstrous bureaucracy to manage it. Prices went up and up, while strikes and protests were crudely put down. There were riots in Lima, where the newspapers were closed for a time. A short diversionary war, fought with Ecuador over the border area where oil had been discovered, ended in stalemate. The country was in an awful mess. The annual rate of inflation went up to 5,000 per cent. Even the currency had deteriorated. Banknotes had been so long in circulation that they became as ragged and brittle as autumn leaves, and so filthy it was like handling and pocketing dung. So few coins were available that one regularly received change in kind: chewing gum, candy or postage stamps. And the stamps started coming without glue so there was a terrible hassle with the paste wheel at the post office.

At the university I predictably sank to the depth that suited me best, that is, where I felt free and anonymous, which was in the company of seedy, part-time students and hangers-on who maintained themselves by trading in cocaine. At this level of society, where there are no friends, only alliances, I often heard casual, murderous references to the Calderóns and to other patrician families – how good it would be to kill them, kidnap them, chop them up, and torture them for their crimes. It was simply assumed that anybody with money or power should be eliminated.

I was horrified to learn that Uncle Joshua headed a list of people to be executed when the revolution came. At the same time it was hard not to sympathize with those who wanted to destroy a hierarchy that had for centuries denied human rights to the majority of native Peruvians.

To stay out of trouble I kept my head down and my mouth shut. I listened, but I didn't take sides. Such a noncommittal attitude was not an admirable one, but it enabled me to survive. This was the time when graffiti was being scrawled on all the walls of the lecture halls:

PAN PARA TODO*
EL PUEBLO MUERE DE HAMBRE†

*Bread for the people   †This country is dying of hunger

29

The university, I soon discovered, was less a place of learning than a forum for political debate. Student strikes and demonstrations were common, and the police kept a water cannon permanently parked outside the main gate, to put a damper on riots. Uncle Joshua, who was a member of the Board of Regents, had warned me that I might find the professors a bit left-wing, but nothing could have prepared me for the legendary Dr Morales who taught Peruvian history to freshmen. In his book, entitled *Xenophobic Dogs* and a bestseller on campus, he openly called for nothing less than the wholesale upheaval and removal of Spanish culture from Peru. The book was inspired by his experiences in China during the Cultural Revolution, and in it he predicted a catastrophe that would trigger radical social, political, economic and cultural changes; these would sweep over Peru, ridding the country of Spanish influence and transforming it into the pure Indian republic that it was before the Conquest. He chose Mao's China as his model because of its similarities with Peru. Both countries were semi-colonial and semi-feudal, with a mass of illiterate peasants abused for centuries by an elite, foreign minority.

Dr Morales, or Comrade Osvaldo, as he came to be known, was a fiery orator. A tiny man with the rage of a bull, he spoke, or rather screamed his message in a high-pitched whine that kept us on the edge of our seats. Every now and then he would desist from his Marxist chant to show us how to make a Molotov cocktail, or how to hurl a stick of dynamite with a llama-hair sling, the weapon of Indian herdsmen. Naturally, the students were mesmerized. He used to enter the lecture hall with a queer, stiff-legged gait. His teeth were clenched, and his face was knotted in a perpetual scowl. He spoke to no one and looked neither right nor left, but during the lecture he used to glance my way every now and then. I guess he was fascinated by my weird *mestizo* looks, which probably epitomized for him everything that was wrong with Peru. Those piercing black eyes seemed to stare right through me. Everybody said he was a genius, but he looked like the Devil to me. I could almost see his cloven hooves stamping behind the lectern, and his little tail twitching peevishly. Withdrawn and secretive by nature, he had no personal contact with the freshmen and only associated with an older militant group of left-wing students, known as 'storm troopers'.

It came out later that Dr Morales was busy setting up a cell structure among students that was to make his terrorist organization virtually impenetrable. Even while he was lecturing he was laying the groundwork for guerrilla warfare, training student lieutenants and using field trips and research projects to recruit members of impoverished Indian communities. His land-reform projects had become so popular among the Indians that 'liberated areas' and communes had already been established in some remote parts of Puno Province. These regions were so rugged and inaccessible that the Indians there had never been conquered, not even by the Incas. At the same time, it was rumoured, those students loyal to him were leaving the university to infiltrate the police and the military. They took jobs with the railroad and the utility companies in order to learn how to destroy them. They were serving as spies everywhere.

Conditions in Peru were ripe for a Maoist-type revolution, he told us. His plan was to organize the rural populations, then move into the shantytowns in order to isolate and choke off the cities. His commando units were already 'playing games' by blowing up electric pylons, which caused power cuts and plunged Lima and Arequipa into darkness. It was a campaign that would take decades. He was waiting for a democratically elected administration to take office before launching an all-out war, because he wanted to show the world that the whole system of government in Peru, civilian or military, was rotten.

The University of San Agustín, Uncle Joshua told me, was one of the oldest in the western hemisphere and prided itself on being a place for freedom of speech. Even so, it seemed incredible to me that the Board of Regents allowed Dr Morales to preach revolution and even to organize one right under their noses. Either they were blandly tolerant of him or they didn't know what was going on. It was only when he suggested that the university itself must be burned to the ground that he was given the sack.

In his farewell lecture, Dr Morales declared his movement to be the vanguard of world revolution. 'We are thousands,' he said, raising his clenched fist. 'We are the fundamentalists of the armed left. We are fighting to enter a new historical stage of Marxism because everywhere, in other revolutions, men have seized power only to dominate the people. When this new era comes,' he screeched gleefully, 'the Russians and the North Americans will attack us together because they will find our true Communism intolerable. They will attack us but they cannot defeat us. The Chinese Mountains will be our stronghold from which we will begin our long march to freedom.'

He disappeared and was not seen in public again. Soon afterwards the number of students at the university began to fall mysteriously. Young men and women were dropping out and drifting to the countryside where, it was reported, they were being indoctrinated into what now began to be called the Shining Path, or Sixteenth of December movement. This was the date in 1533 that the last ruling Inca, Atahualpa, had been garrotted by the Spanish at Cajamarca. Dr Morales was the founder and leader.

To some, Dr Morales and his followers were passionate idealists, determined to redress injustices going back 400 years. To others they were a bunch of savage outlaws. They shunned publicity and appeared not to depend on outside support. Their favourite weapon was dynamite which was plentiful in Peru, a mining nation. Anything connected with modern life – schools, dams, hydroelectric plants – they went out of their way to destroy. Near Cuzco they pushed a boulder on to a passing freight train loaded with sacks of wheat; then they looted the train and distributed the food to the poor. Operating in columns of up to fifty young men and women, they blew up police stations, attacked tanks and banks, killed policemen, and issued death warrants for government officials. Their victims were found in mass graves. Many people were shocked that women were involved. One force consisting entirely of women overran a government post near Azangaro, the biggest town in central Puno Province, killing six soldiers and hacking the bodies to bits. Operating among the poorest Puno hamlets that had been bedevilled by drought followed by the worst floods this century, these self-styled Robin Hoods doled out 600 rustled cattle to peasants. Local mayors and village chiefs, terrified by the death threats, either quit or fled.

The army was obliged to adopt a severe counterinsurgency strategy to oppose the guerrillas. This involved the use of terror, including kidnappings, torture and the summary executions of suspects. More and more mass graves were found. Far from achieving the expected victory over a ruthless enemy, however, by employing brutal reprisal tactics the army only increased guerrilla support.

As the economic situation worsened, lawlessness returned to the countryside. Bizarre incidents began to be reported in the newspapers. It was as though every discontented element in the country was jumping on the bandwagon to outdo the other by some outrageous act. At Machu Picchu, a naked savage carrying a machete stepped from behind a sacrificial altar, lopped off the head of an American tourist, and ran away with it. Terrified by death threats, the number of foreign archaeologists working in the Sierra dropped off sharply, and the International Potato Center moved its high-altitude research station from Peru's highlands to Ecuador. Near Puerto Maldonado in Madre de Dios Province, a tribe of Christianized Indians suddenly turned on the missionaries who had lived among them for years, and ate them. The Shining Path stole Atahualpa's golden funeral hands from the archaeological museum in Lima, declaring the ruling junta unworthy to be guardians of such a relic. In Tingo Maria the daughter of Count Bardolini, the Italian ambassador, was kidnapped. She was held prisoner in a jungle cave for two weeks until the ransom was paid. Upon being freed she showed symptoms of the so-called Stockholm Syndrome – a tendency of some hostages to sympathize with their captors. At a press conference she caused a sensation by describing the experience as 'exhilarating', and her captors as 'beautiful people fighting for a noble cause'. 'I have lived with the Shining Path,' she proclaimed to reporters. 'I have seen the union among them, the solidarity. I have talked with them and know that they fight with conviction and high morale. Everybody should be kidnapped in order to understand how Peru may be restored to that agricultural paradise that it was at the time of the Incas.' According to Cardinal Castrillon Robles y Damas, who was present at her release, she 'warmly embraced her captors before leaving them'. Miss Bardolini was promptly put on the first plane back to Italy.

Uncle Joshua and I discussed these events. The sympathy that he expressed for the guerrillas amazed me.

'Did you know,' he said, 'that this Shining Path organization has called for the country to be given back to the Indians?'

'Dr Morales has also vowed to destroy every Spanish family and the culture they represent.'

'I know it sounds strange, but I believe I can talk to him and perhaps avoid the catastrophe he predicts. No, I feel an almost mystical, spiritual accord with him and his followers, though I deplore their brutal tactics.' He sighed. 'But I suppose I understand them. I understand how reasonable and intelligent men can become fanatics by being denied what are unquestionably their rights for years and years and years.'

Uncle Joshua made me swear to keep my family connection a secret. Rosalinda, he told me, had been sent to school in England to allay fears of kidnapping following her exposure in the newspapers. I lived alone in a room off campus and was careful to choose a circuitous route whenever I went to the Calderón house. I don't think my shady acquaintances ever guessed that I ate nearly every Sunday lunch with The Cork. They no more associated me with Charlie than North Americans would suspect a black man called Washington of being a descendant of the Founding Father. My Indian face was my cover; they knew my name but not my identity.

Nor, for that matter, did I. Part of me was a Christian who never prayed. Part was pagan removed from Eden. My father was a lecherous missionary – odious breed. My mother came from a tribe of savages who a generation ago would have devoured his testicles and reduced his head to the size of a cricket ball. To my adoptive parents I was a conundrum.

Basically I was just another member of the rootless and confused whose shantytowns surround every city in Peru. It was beginning to dawn on me that, despite my privileges, there would never be any place for me in this country. I had a foot in both camps – Peru's ruling élite and the students sworn to smash it – but belonged to neither.

Demoralized by my situation, I lost interest in my studies, cut classes and failed the exams. Because of this double life, I made no friends at the university. My only friend was Uncle Joshua who, in Rosalinda's absence, treated me like a son. He had confided in me his family's darkest secrets and his vision for Peru, but sympathy for both sides prevented me from responding like a loyal son. I was afraid to tell him what his fate would be if the revolution succeeded. Guilt held me back, just as it did from admitting that I coveted Juanpablo farm.

He invited me to Juanpablo many times. I spent all my holidays there. Together we took long walks through the orchards. Life on the farm was straightforward and healthy. Water ran in channels to all the thirsty roots, and I felt nourished, too. Like the little children who surrounded him, I wanted to give him big hugs. It was on one of these walks that he disclosed to me that he had agreed to run for the presidency.

To head off what looked to be a spontaneous revolt breaking out all over the country, the colonels had suddenly announced a return to democracy. Elections would be held within three months. The political parties were taken completely by surprise. Charlie's old coalition, the Christian Democrats, came up with the idea of nominating Uncle Joshua. The colonels' disastrous economic policies had set the clock back twenty years. With so little time to campaign the CDU calculated that, by putting forward the name of another Calderón, ignoring the present (the country's ills were too numerous to recount; to talk about them would only demoralize the electorate), and harking back to the good old days under Charlie, they might pull off the election.

The election itself was nearly wrecked by the guerrillas. They were now financing their revolution by acting as middlemen between the Indians of the Upper Huallaga Valley (hitherto a peaceful coffee-growing area), who cultivated seventy per cent of the world's coca supply, and the Columbians. They were beginning to usurp the Columbians' role by refining the plant into cocaine and smuggling it directly to the USA.

Their aim was to provoke the military Government into taking drastic counterinsurgency measures that would drive the Indians into the arms of the Shining Path. In some villages, they threatened to chop off the thumb of every person who voted. The mayor of Chuquibambilla near Cuzco was giving a speech urging people to vote when terrorists hiding on the church tower sprayed the marketplace with machine-gun fire, killing eleven and wounding eighty-three.

The Government braced itself for the worst. The army patrolled the streets of Arequipa in armoured cars. By night, bomb blasts rocked the outlying areas as the guerrillas sought to cut the power supply. Helicopters whizzed overhead, and we heard the rattle of machine guns. The mayor promised free transportation to the polls and assigned policemen to accompany buses bringing Indians in from the *barriadas* to vote.

In the midst of this war-like atmosphere, Uncle Joshua's soft-spoken manner and shy smile came across on television like a breath of fresh air. Here was the face of democracy, and he became a celebrity overnight. Unlike the other candidates, he didn't make any wild promises or outline any grandiose schemes. His platform was to reduce the size of the State and make it more efficient. He wanted to return the companies and banks that had been nationalized or confiscated by the colonels to the private sector, and to scale down the bureaucracy. He intended to encourage foreign investment in order to create new jobs, and to re-establish ties with the International Monetary Fund. But mainly he talked about farming, and he knew what he was talking about.

'Peruvians want to vote,' he said in a TV address to the nation the night before the election, 'because we are faced with open war. Either democracy wins this election, or the Shining Path takes control. There is no way of reaching an agreement with them at this time. We are losing our fear because we are almost losing our country.'

The entire country breathed a sigh of relief when, after several weeks of violence and bloodshed, my uncle Joshua was elected President of Peru.

6

The situation calmed down and, a month after the election and just a week before Christmas, Rosalinda, who had been absent nearly four years, abruptly and without notice returned home. She had been, to use her own word, 'rusticated' from her school in England for sneaking off to attend a soccer match between England and the touring Peruvian team.

Late one night there was a heavy thumping noise on the stairs outside my room, followed by a loud knock on the door. I opened it, and there was my cousin, dressed in plus-fours, turtle-neck sweater and tweed jacket.

'James,' she said, 'I know it's late and we don't know each other, but there was no one else I could turn to.'

Crowding behind her, like primitive statues excluded from the light, were two swarthy Indians.

'Please meet my friends, Sinesio and Amador. This is my cousin James.'

I shook hands with the Indians. Physical contact briefly animated them. When our fingers touched, their wooden faces flickered to life.

'Are we disturbing you? I promise we'll only stay a minute.'

'I was just doing some packing. Come on in.'

It was as though a signal had been given. I stood by the door while a huge tyre was rolled into the room.

'I know this is a terrible imposition, and I promise it'll be gone in a day or two. It was heading for the city dump, you see. Mother's orders. She's mounting a massive house-cleaning operation before Daddy's inauguration and the move to Lima. I had to perform this rescue mission in the middle of the night.'

Rosalinda pointed to an empty corner where the tyre was laid flat. Her companions sat down on it.

At first I couldn't imagine what Rosalinda was doing in the company of these two desperadoes. She wore Scottish tweeds and a deerstalker; they had on ragged ponchos and woollen Sierra caps with earflaps. On her feet were English walking shoes with leather tassels; their cracked and dirty feet were shod with sandals made out of old rubber tyres. Her father had just been elected President of Peru. Sinesio, I was told, sometimes shovelled coal at the depot; Amador sometimes drove trucks over the Andes. Her features, the pale skin, soft, deep-set eyes like her father's, and black hair, were pure Andalusian. Their unsmiling expressions came right off a Chimu vase, or could have been sculpted in stone. They were without doubt two of the toughest-looking hombres I had ever laid eyes on. Maybe they were her bodyguards; maybe they worshipped her; their faces were complete blanks. Indian eyes flicked suspiciously over my books, my papers, my desk, my bed and other trappings of civilization.

'Ever since Uncle George and Aunt Grace found you in the jungle, you've been quite a celebrity in our family,' Rosalinda said. 'A blond Indian – you sounded terribly romantic.'

'What were you expecting – young Tarzan? Or the missing link?'

'You've got a chip on your shoulder, too. What's the jungle like? I know everyone must ask you the same question.'

'It was home for the first eight years of my life, but I can hardly remember it any more.'

'Was it dangerous? We all think it must be, with those snakes and spiders, and slimy things crawling around.'

'The jungle was a pleasant place to live . . . for children.'

'Do you miss it?'

'Sometimes. When I lie awake in the middle of the night, wondering what I'm going to do with my life, I can hear the river. All the children could swim like minnows. We never wore clothes. We spent our days diving and playing games, sliding down the rapids, playing hide and seek among the rocks and waterfalls.'

'Do you think you would ever go back and live there one day?'

'There's no place for me there . . . or here, for that matter.'

She regarded me thoughtfully, and then replied, 'I can tell that you're a lonely boy.'

'You're the first person to have said that.'

'But you shouldn't feel lonely. You must think of my family as your family. Daddy talks about you as though you were his son.'

'He's been very kind, but your mother disapproves of the colour of my skin. I could tell by the look in her eye the first day we met.'

'That's her old-fashioned prejudice. You'll have to forgive her.'

'Why should I forgive racial prejudice when it's what has been ruining this country for the past 400 years?'

She seemed taken aback by my outburst. 'I don't think there's anything anyone can do or say to change it.'

'The Shining Path is trying to change it.'

'Are you on their side?' she asked uneasily.

'No, but I think Charlie would rather have me around as a houseboy than sit down at Sunday lunch with me.'

For Rosalinda, Charlie was sacred. She thought for a minute about how to reply, then decided to change the subject.

'Is it true that Indian boys and girls wander off into the jungle and make love any time they like?'

'If they do, everyone knows about it, and they get married very young. Life in the jungle is anything but romantic.'

'Why did they torture you?'

'Because my hair is blond and my eyes are blue.'

'How barbaric!' Rosalinda turned to her companions. 'Sinesio and Amador are my former team-mates – the only ones I could find. The others are scattered – in the army or gone to Lima for work. Eduardito, our star, the one we had high hopes for, the one I expected to be on the Peruvian team that came to London, broke a leg in training and never played again.' Her eyes had a faraway look. 'It's such a pity. He was the most graceful athlete I've ever seen. I got all the publicity because

40

I was a girl and because of my family, but he was the star, and the most naturally gifted soccer player in Arequipa. He's a bandit now. There's a price on his head, and he's hiding out in the mountains somewhere. The army is after him. Charlie showed me a newspaper clipping.'

'Charlie must be glad you're back,' I said. 'Is he talking again?'

'Now everybody wishes he'd shut up. He's taking me fishing tomorrow. We're not coming back until the day before Christmas. You're going to spend Christmas with us, aren't you? Good. It will be our last family Christmas before Daddy takes office. I hear you're going to be leaving us soon.'

'Yes. I didn't get my degree, so I'm going to go back to Santa Cruz on New Year's Day.'

'And miss the inauguration?'

'I haven't seen my mother and father in over a year.'

'Won't Uncle George and Aunt Grace be coming to Lima for the inauguration?'

'I don't think so.'

'Daddy hasn't seen him in twenty years, and I've never met him.'

'You'll have to go to Santa Cruz to do that.'

'That's sad, but I respect his independence. Daddy says he offered you a job in Lima, but you turned him down.'

'I don't think I'd fit into Lima society, do you? Besides, I promised my father I'd come home and help him with his business.'

'Oh. And we've only just met. My birthday's on the first of January, too. Listen, there's a dream I've got to tell you about. A nightmare about Charlie I had in England. It worried me so much, it's one of the reasons I came back. You're in it, even though I didn't know you. Daddy wrote about you in his letters. James this, James that. You know, it made me a little jealous, because you seemed to be taking my place in my father's affections. Do you want to hear?'

I was amused by her honesty. 'Sure.'

'You, Charlie and I were standing on the edge of a vast lake in a frozen landscape. Beyond the lake were the Chinese

41

Mountains. That's Charlie's word for the Andes. He calls them that because they're so remote and inaccessible, and because the Indians who live up there lead lives so completely removed from our own that they might as well be on the other side of the world. Anyway,' she went on, 'to get back to the dream, the ground was as hard as a rock, there wasn't a cloud in sight, and the air rang with cold. Charlie walked out on the lake. The ice was at least a foot thick and dark blue, almost black. He walked far out while you and I remained on the shore, watching. Suddenly the ice around Charlie began to give way. It broke up slowly, and he sank from sight, without a splash. The water received him soundlessly, like oil. I was screaming, "God! God! God!" but I couldn't, for some reason, look right or left. I didn't know if you had run for planks or dogs. Then I woke up, and my heart was pounding,' she finished breathlessly.

'Dr Morales calls the Andes the Chinese Mountains, too. He was my history teacher at San Agustín before he disappeared. He had a different explanation, though. He said it was because the Indians originally came from Asia. You know, they migrated across the Bering Strait thousands of years ago and fanned out through the Americas.'

'I didn't know that. But isn't this Morales the leader of the Shining Path?'

'That's right, and their philosophy is Maoist because he was a student in China during the Cultural Revolution.'

'Do you think the Shining Path will win?'

'No, because your father proved that democracy still works in Peru by winning the election fair and square.'

'When I was in England,' she said sadly, 'I prayed every night he would lose.'

'Why?'

'Daddy's not a politician. He's too kind-hearted for politics. Charlie loves a fight, not Daddy. He should stick to farming.'

7

Three days later, while he was netting a trout, Charlie slipped from the boulder where he was fishing. Rosalinda, who was casting her line a few yards upstream, watched helplessly as her grandfather tumbled into the water. Scrambling frantically over rocks and fallen trees, she ran to save him. He clung briefly to a rock before being swept away by the current. The river was in full spate and icy cold from melting snow. Half dead from shock and exhausted from struggling in the freezing torrent, she finally managed to drag his body ashore a quarter of a mile downstream. Everybody said it was a miracle she hadn't drowned with him.

Christmas was cancelled. Summer was just beginning, but the weather turned cold, and it began to snow. The flakes were falling in the cemetery and beginning to fill the pit where Charlie would be placed. On a cold and snowy morning, the last day of the year, the Calderón clan gathered for the state funeral.

In the cathedral, the resonant words of Archbishop Nineth de Cisneros rolled like waves across the black sea of mourners. 'Death is merely a horizon. This horizon is the limit of our vision. We are able to see no further than the horizon. . . .'

Rosalinda squeezed my hand. 'Horizons,' she whispered through her veil. 'I want mine to be flat and green. I'm sick of these mountains, this cold and this snow. James, can I come with you to Santa Cruz?'

Even through her veil she looked beautiful. Spanish girls know how to wear black. In spite of the solemnity of the occasion, everyone was staring at her. She had been away four years, and they were all dying to know what she looked like.

'Are you crazy?' I hissed. 'Of course you can't. You've just come back from England. You've been gone for ages. You can't go running off now. Your father needs you. The whole family does.'

'Do you know that I have twenty-one first cousins and every last one of them turned up for the funeral? I've never seen such exaggerated mourning. I mean, you'd think he was Bolivar. I don't want to talk about Charlie day in and day out to people I don't know. They're like a crowd of black vultures waiting around for a piece of the cake.'

'Is there a cake?' I asked.

'I wish there was! Charlie may have done a lot of things we're not particularly proud of, but one thing he didn't do when he was in office was fill his pockets. All there is is Juanpablo farm, and that goes to Daddy.'

'What about my father?' I asked. 'Does he get anything?'

'Well, I suppose he must.' Rosalinda seemed surprised by my question. 'He's been away so long I just never thought about it. I suppose Juanpablo . . . must belong equally to both of them.'

'Listen,' I said. 'This is a crucial time for your father. You can't walk out on him now. He'll want all his family around him; he'll need your support. If you go gallivanting around the countryside, it'll only worry and distract him at a time when he needs to concentrate on some big problems. His judgement is going to affect the future of Peru.'

'Listen, cousin. . . .' Tears were streaming down her cheeks. 'I tried to save him, but I couldn't. Now *I* need to be saved . . . from this grief. I don't want to dress in black. I don't want to go to the cemetery every day. I'm going to be eighteen tomorrow. Please let me come with you.'

'The earth is a rolling orb,' intoned the Archbishop. 'It spins inexorably from day to day. As surely as the dawn follows night we will finally emerge into His glorious radiance, and so to eternal life. . . .'

At the cemetery gates I parted from Rosalinda and the family with the promise that I would visit the house in the evening to say goodbye. It had stopped snowing and the sun had come out. Donning my dark glasses, I made my way through the white stone streets – volcanic stones tumbled repeatedly by earthquakes – to the Plaza de Armas for my daily ration of *ceviche*. It's raw fish marinated in lime juice, and comes with raw onion rings, coriander, hot pepper and a slab of sweet potato and a chunk of Indian corn to neutralize the pepper. Aside from Sunday lunches with my cousins, I had lived on little else for three years. Thus fortified, I crossed the square to buy a newspaper from a kiosk beneath the arcades, dived into a corner bar for a glass of *pisco* and, feeling a little drunk, sat down on a park bench to read Charlie's obituary.

Almost immediately a haggard, rat-like figure in a grimy raincoat slid in beside me. He declared himself to be a former student at the university. He seemed vaguely familiar; I recalled seeing his Indian face somewhere before. Maybe it was on a pot in the archaeological museum. I thought he wanted a handout. For a few minutes he babbled obsessively about the weather, history, politics and the universe. The air was cold, but the sun burned fiercely in a cloudless sky. The city seemed to have emptied of people. Suddenly the student, taking my arm in a fierce grip, feverishly demanded to know what I thought of the future of the world.

I yawned. Maybe it was the altitude that did it, or the *pisco*. I closed my eyes, breathed in the good mountain air, felt the hot sun on my back, and shrugged.

The student glared at me. 'Well?'

'I don't mean to be rude,' I said, 'but I've just been to a funeral. I don't feel like discussing the future of the world right now.'

Without thinking, I pointed to the black-framed photo on the front page of the newspaper beneath the headline:

THE CORK GOES UNDER

And there was Charlie, not ten yards away, hanging on for dear life to a rearing, bucking stallion (symbol of the unruly republic) and madly waving a pistol. The statue had been caught in crossfire during the Peasant Revolution, and had received a few superficial wounds. An epaulette had been shot

45

away, and the reins blasted out of his hands. Charlie had been proud of that statue. Having been shot at so many times in his stormy career, he was pleased to know that he was still in the line of fire.

The front page was devoted to the Calderón family – the deceased President, the President-elect, and all their kin. The student grabbed the newspaper from me and pointed to a photo of myself standing between Charlie and Uncle Joshua.

He stared at me, open-mouthed. 'You – kin to The Cork?'

Before I could answer, he stopped his jiggling, jumped to his feet, and made off without another word. The sun simultaneously disappeared behind a solitary cloud, and the temperature seemed to drop several degrees. A shiver passed through me as a policeman carrying a sub-machine-gun materialized from a pocket of shadow and followed the student.

On the way back to my room, something made me pause before a wall poster to examine once more the photos of 'terrorists' that I had first seen in the post office and which were now beginning to appear at the university and other public places where they were permanently and prominently displayed. Among the young men and women branded as 'assassins', 'anarchists', 'arsonists', and so on, was the frozen face of the student I had just been talking to in the park. His name was Pedro, his alias was 'The Armadillo', and he was wanted for 'manufacturing bombs and causes'. Now I remembered him: he had been one of Dr Morales's 'storm troopers' who had escorted the professor to and from his lectures.

Next to The Armadillo, the fierce but fuzzy countenance of Eduardito, Rosalinda's former team-mate, stared at me from above a row of numbers. He was wanted dead or alive in Puno Province for 'disruption, destruction, extortion and rape'.

8

Thus, with a belly full of *pisco*, I saw in the New Year from a stone bench in Cathedral Square. Like imprisoned animals that throw themselves recklessly against the bars of their cage, the elongated shadows of the bell ringers were leaping against the walls of the belfry. The great bells were clanging, and the sound was reverberating down the white stone streets of Arequipa. It carried through the cold mountain night to the parched and irrigated valleys and abandoned terraced hillsides, repository of agricultural secrets that had remained unshared for 400 years since the Conquest.

As the bells rang out, firecrackers exploded. Rockets hissed upwards, and expired in the night. The village churches could be heard responding with pitiful clanks as I left the square and wobbled down a shiny stone street that had once been part of an Inca highway. The cobbles, round and glossy, had been worn smooth by the tread of a million faithful shuffling feet.

'Shuffling towards what?' I wondered out loud.

'Shuffling along this shining path towards the dawn of a world revolution,' a voice replied.

Someone was walking beside me.

Short, the top of his head came to the level of my shoulder. Dressed in the nondescript baggy brown suit that city Indians seem to favour, he was, I thought, the hustler who had attempted to sell me cocaine several times before. I was about to say, 'No. No, hombre, not tonight.' But he caught hold of my elbow and whispered, 'Tonight I am your host. It is New Year's Eve and I will buy you a drink.'

Giving me a light tap on the shoulder, he pointed to a *chicha* bar I'd never noticed before.

When I hesitated, he shoved me down a flight of steps and prodded me through a door.

The place was dark and ill-lit, like a cave or cellar. The floor was the earth, with sawdust scattered on it. A number of chickens wandered about. The only female in the place was a *chichera* – a decrepit Indian woman in a shawl and bowler hat who for ten cents offered large glasses of the horrible brew from a metal bucket. *Chicha* is made by the Indians who chew up corn kernels, and spit them back into a bowl. The saliva makes the contents ferment. It's a bubbly and sour drink that Indians pour down until they drop, but I don't like it.

'All friends,' my host was saying, as he raised his glass and saluted the sullen, poncho-clad lumps of clay that jammed the booths. 'All my friends.' He emptied the glass. 'Therefore all your friends. Eh, Calderón? All these Indians are your friends.'

It was a simple logic, and one which I was almost prepared to accept. Once the frontier into Indian territory is crossed, one encounters immediately a looseness about time, a shoulder-shrugging idleness and fatality. But drops of blood and broken glass glistened on the zinc bar; among my 'friends' my host apparently included in his sweeping gesture a fellow lying face down on the sawdust floor.

My host, who called himself Rodrigo, claimed to be an ex-professor of anthropology who had sided with the losing faction during the Peasant Revolution. In reality it was the elusive Dr Morales.

He had grown a beard since I last saw him. It had come out in patches and didn't connect with his moustache. At the university his bushy head of hair had earned him the nickname *La Oveja* (The Sheep). He and I had one thing in common that nothing could disguise – the despised *mestizo* look. His scruffy, unkempt appearance was belied by the intensity in his eyes. They glowered at me from the heavy Indian features like two obsidian beads.

*The Bar where Brave Men Cry

'My people who puzzle the gringo, friend, possess many conflicting characteristics – *mucho* energy and implacable inertia, bright-eyed alertness and blind fatalism. We can be as nimble as the vicuña or as sluggish as prisoners dragging chains, no? We are quick to laugh and joke over nothing, yet you will say that sadness marks our faces, our art, our entire civilization. Our industriousness, our endurance, and our ability to labour under very bad conditions have impressed the gringo, who has not failed to exploit us. The presence of strangers in our land confounds us utterly. Why? Ever since the Spaniard first set foot on our shore we have been paralysed, unable to move one way or another. Yet from that time, meester, we have changed our ways not at all. We keep to the mountains and preserve our language.'

Perhaps Uncle Joshua was right – it was an obstinate waiting game they were collectively playing – waiting for the white man to go away.

'What do you say?' He stamped hard on my foot. 'Do you agree or not?'

'Ouch! What'd you do that for? What do you want from me?'

He downed his drink and winked at me. 'Just a little chat.'

The one on the floor dragged himself to his feet, wiped the blood from his face, and grinned sheepishly. It was The Armadillo.

'What happened to him?' I asked.

'He couldn't remember your first name.'

'How could he have known it?'

'James, ain't it? The newspaper says you're George's son, which makes our new president-elect your uncle.'

'If you read it in the newspaper, it must be true.'

'My condolences for your grandfather. A fitting end for a guy who spent most of his time fishing, no?'

There was a chorus of coarse guffaws from the Indians. They were packed so tightly into the booths they seemed welded together. Two of them stood with their backs to the door to prevent anyone from entering or leaving the cantina. I was Dr Morales's prisoner.

'Why, your granddaddy was one of the most famous presidents we've ever had,' he went on. 'He whipped Ecuador, didn't he? He was the capitalists' friend. He invited every Yankee corporation to Peru and sold them the mineral rights, the oil exploration rights, the grasslands, the timber. In return for what? That's what I'd like to know. Why, The Cork must have stashed away a pile of gold as high as El Misti.'

'I'll tell you one thing,' I said. 'If The Cork was anything he was honest. He never took a bribe or a pay-off from anybody.'

'He also murdered more Indians than anyone since the time Pizarro and his band of ravenous pig farmers stole our land. Oh, Peru just loves The Cork and his capitalist kin. You do look kind of familiar. . . . You are his kin, ain't you?'

Wearing an expression of inquisitive hatred, Dr Morales examined my face. 'You sure are a funny-looking fellow,' he added. 'You sure you got the right one, Pedro?' he asked. 'Hey, boy, how did you get to be George's son? Did he find you under a bush or did he take a roll in the hay with an Indian girl? Now, The Cork wouldn't have approved of an Indian in the family, would he? Ah! Ha ha! Is that why your daddy is the black sheep of the family? Is that why he stays in Santa Cruz and never comes home to Juanpablo?'

'I don't think it's any of your business,' I said.

'That farm ought to belong to you one day, but the Calderóns won't let you have it, will they?'

Dr Morales's discovery of my secret obsession hit me like a boxer's fist. I took an involuntary step backwards, but the grim-looking, red-eyed men guarding the door made me stop.

'And now here comes the bumbling, saintly Joshua, campaigning on a family name so famous that he hardly has to roll out of the hammock to win the election.'

'He wants to talk to you,' I said.

'Oh he does, does he? President Calderón wishes to talk to me!' he screeched at the booths. He was answered by sullen laughter. He pinched a piece of my neck flesh between his thumb and forefinger and squeezed hard. 'Doesn't he know it's too late for talking?' he said between his teeth. 'Doesn't the ignoramus even know that?'

'Ow! That hurts! It's never too late to talk,' I said, turning my head away from his *chicha* breath.

'It's too late for my father and his two brothers entombed since the sixteenth of December, 1964 at the bottom of El Gordo!'

A chill went down my spine when he said that. Dr Morales had named his terrorist organization not only, as was popularly believed, for the date of Atahualpa's death, but also for the El Gordo mine disaster. How he must hate the Calderóns!

'That wasn't his fault,' I said. 'It was Charlie's.'

He let me go. 'So the saintly Joshua has washed his hands of that, too, has he?'

'He agrees with the Shining Path on many issues, mainly land reform. What he doesn't agree with is your violence. He understands it, but he can't agree to it.'

'Land reform! Hear that, compadres? Land reform was an issue of the sixties, not 1990!' His voice was like the sound fingernails make, scraping a blackboard. 'What a fine up-to-date president he's going to make. We hate Joshua worse than the colonels.'

'But why? How can you. . . ?'

'Because he thinks he can go on talking while people starve! Talking is over. When you see him again, tell him that the days of talking about land reform are over for ever.'

'I don't think I'll see him again. If it'll make you feel any better,' I said, 'I'm going home. I'm leaving for Santa Cruz in the morning.'

'Perfect!' he shouted. 'Give him some *chicha*, Pedro.'

The Armadillo slid a glass the size of a flowerpot along the bar.

'Not for me, thanks.'

'The whole world applauded his election, didn't it? The President of the United States and the President of the Soviet Union sent their warmest congratulations. You can tell him that the Shining Path also rejoices in his victory.'

'I don't understand. . . .'

'Because he's going to show the world how corrupt and irrelevant a democratic government is for our country.' He scrutinized me. 'Tell me, sonny . . . where have you and I seen each other before?'

'I was in your class at the university.'

'So you were! How could I forget a face like that? Well, in that case we're going to let you go home, meester capitalist friend. Give my regards to Wall Street! And let me tell you one more thing. A little piece of friendly advice. There's only one way for you to have Juanpablo farm.'

'How?' I could not resist asking.

Smiling, he drew his forefinger across his neck.

9

In the streets adjacent to the Plaza de Armas, the Indians had set up trestle tables and benches, where by the light of a few flickering lamps they offered *pisco* and roast hedgehog and assorted boiled potatoes. They were not drunk – this was not their New Year entering; they were just there, dominating the scene with their sad, numbing presence.

'Ugh!' I choked on a purple potato and signalled the woman for another *pisco* to wash it down. My mind was still reeling from my encounter with Dr Morales. Like Mephistopheles, he was able to see into the recesses of my disordered soul. His intimate knowledge of the Calderón family could only mean that he had studied them for years while plotting revenge for the El Gordo mine disaster.

Somewhere someone was playing *chicha* music with flute and drum as the Indians moved silently down starlit streets. These quiet, open-faced people were marked by a dullness that perhaps was a mask for instinctive intelligence. The Inca empire was a consolidation of many cultures. It produced goods and wealth and was supremely organized. Gold was only valued for ornaments. There were great public works. Then the empire fell – at a touch – like a huge house of cards. Now there was nothing but sadness, this immense sadness. One could only guess at the sensitivity of their race from the music, which was dangerously mournful and fragile.

The Armadillo, I knew, had followed me from the cantina. I was being watched. He was out there somewhere, among the hundreds of Indians who swarmed in the uncertain light, squabbling in whispers over llama foetuses and alligator oil. I glanced at my watch and looked into the sky. There was the Southern Cross and the Milky Way flowing like a luminous river through the night. It was one o'clock in the morning; a cold wind was blowing down from the mountains.

A fuzzy white puppy was gnawing on my shoe. The owner of the dog, an Indian child, was standing at my side and tentatively squeezing my arm.

I looked from the doll-like face to my once-shiny shoes. The puppy was growling fiercely and shaking its head. It had loosened one of my shoelaces and had begun a tug of war. The owner, who led his pet about by a string, was insistently poking me in the ribs.

It was Wilfredito, Santusa Izquierda's boy. Santusa was Rosalinda's maid; she and her son slept together in a closet under the stairs outside Rosalinda's room.

'What is it, Wilfredito?'

Wilfredito went on squeezing my arm. He was evidently waiting. Even the puppy had wearied of its game. It was sitting on its haunches, wagging its tail and looking expectantly at me. I got to my feet, and took Wilfredito's hand. He allowed the dog to lead the way. We proceeded slowly and hesitantly, as the dog inspected the ground ahead of us.

Leaving the arcaded plaza, we entered a long narrow corridor of a street overhung by the high white rampart of Santa Catalina. Barred windows were spaced far apart. The street opened upon the familiar park with its trees and cathedral and now-silent tower, then closed again as we turned a corner and made our way along the rear of the Calderón house. Wilfredito stopped, the dog sat down and yawned; then a noise made me look up. A light flashed above my head as a window opened. A hand appeared and an object was flung out. The window closed, shutting off the light.

The object, which was white, did not fall directly. It seemed to fly. It floated in a wide arc, passed obliquely through the green glow of a streetlamp, and skidded to a landing on the cobbles, startling the puppy which had been dozing. The dog approached, judiciously placed its paw on the object, and sniffed. Wilfredito retrieved it. It was a paper glider. I unfolded it and read:

Cousin

Why didn't you come as you promised? Are you all right? Are you ill? We waited and waited, and Daddy was worried. It's late now, the doors are bolted, but I shall manage to come out. Please wait for me in the park. I can't come immediately but will be there soon.

R.

10

The park was filling with Indians. Entire families were drifting in from the Plaza de Armas and bedding down for the night. The women, wearing bowler hats and shawls and sweaters, skirts and layers of woollen petticoats, gathered their sleepy children about them. The men paced in circles, then they lay down, tucked blankets around them, drew one breath and fell instantly asleep. The grass was lumpy with sleeping forms, and the park reverted to shadowy silence.

Besides myself, only one other person was awake. A drunken Indian, who had apparently arrived with the others but had not yet found his place, could be seen darting among the trees. Like the others he was bare legged, and he carried a basket. He wore black knee-breeches and sandals fashioned from an old rubber tyre. Beneath a shapeless felt hat he had on a knitted wool cap with earflaps. His poncho, however, was not brown and tattered but bright red and brand new. He moved quickly, like a small animal, but every few yards staggered drunkenly before regaining his balance.

He stumbled to the bench where I was sitting and slumped against me.

'Meester. Poor Indian boy got no place to sleep, no place to go. You give money, no?'

'No.'

'Please meester . . . no mudder and no fadder.'

'Rosalinda, is that you? What do you think you're doing?'

'Sh. We have to be quiet. They may be watching.'

'Who? Who's watching? Are you being followed, too?'

'Your hands are as cold as ice.' She hugged me and kissed me on the cheek. 'Happy New Year! Your teeth are chattering. What's wrong with you? Why don't you speak? You're drunk.'

'Who's watching?'

'The whole family, probably. See those windows? They may seem black and empty, but behind them there are great-aunts, uncles, cousins, relatives I've never heard of or met before. . . . Why didn't you come?'

'I've been wandering the streets all night. I was afraid to go back to my room.'

'Why? What's wrong?'

'I'm being followed.'

'Who by?'

'After the funeral I had this strange conversation with . . . with a criminal. He saw the picture of Charlie and me in the paper. He discovered the family connection. Then he looked at my face and wondered how an Indian could be related to Charlie. Anyway, I didn't come to your house tonight because if he'd seen me going in, he would have known for sure that I'm a member of the family. Rosalinda, please don't tell your father. The last thing I want is for him to find out I'm mixed up with these criminals a few days before he takes office.'

'James, let's not talk here. Daddy may have called the police by now.'

'The police? What for?'

'Isn't it ridiculous? We've got to hide somewhere.'

'But why?'

'Let's go to the cathedral. They'll never think of looking in there.'

We jumped to our feet together.

'And to think, my cousin Teofilio is the Chief of Police.'

'Wait a minute, Rosalinda. I know your cousin is the Chief of Police. So what have you got to be worried about?'

'Not first cousin, second or third cousin once removed, I think. I'm not really worried, not yet. Mother and Daddy are probably sound asleep and think I am, too.'

'The best thing would be for you to go back home before someone discovers you're gone.'

'I've made up my mind – I'm coming with you to Santa Cruz.'

'That's crazy. You can't just go off without telling anyone.'

'I left a note under Daddy's breakfast plate explaining everything. He's going to Juanpablo first thing in the morning with the new farm manager he's hired to run things while he's President. He's taking all the children with him. Mother and I are supposed to stay home and pack. He'll read my note before anyone's awake. I told him that I'm going to mend fences with Uncle George. Our conversation in church this afternoon reminded me that after all these years Daddy still feels very close to him. He feels guilty because he hasn't seen him for ages.'

'Rosalinda, I don't think this is a good idea. The timing is all wrong. Your father has a lot of things on his mind right now. He has the whole country on his mind, not just the family. If you leave now, he's bound to worry about you. Why didn't you just tell him instead of sneaking off in the middle of the night?'

'Mother would have objected.'

'You mean she doesn't want you to associate with me.'

'Well . . .'

I knew what Aunt Mary thought about me and I couldn't stop myself from giving vent to my anger. 'Behind my back she calls me "The Lizard", and you know how she hates lizards – she'll step on them and crush them any chance she gets. She's never been able to swallow the idea of having an Indian nephew, has she? Even an adopted one. In her eyes the family is tarnished by my Indian blood. She calls herself a Christian, but in fact she's incapable of trusting or loving anyone who's racially not exactly the same as herself.'

'You'll have to excuse her, James,' said Rosalinda, clearly upset. 'She's very old-fashioned.'

'You mean she's a snob and a racist and a hypocrite.'

Rosalinda ignored this last remark. 'She would have insisted on writing letters to your parents and that would have delayed the whole thing. Today's my birthday. I don't want to pack. I can't bear the idea of having to face Lima and Lima society just a few days after returning from England. Aren't you going to wish me happy birthday? I'm eighteen. Do you know how

I want to celebrate my independence? By walking naked in the jungle. I'm only joking. Look, I brought my fly rod with me.' She took out a cylindrical case from her basket. 'Charlie always wanted to know which fish fights harder – the trout or the piranha. Now I'm going to find out.'

I should have taken her straight to her house, banged on the door until someone opened, and made sure she was locked up safe and sound inside; but it was New Year's Eve, and I'd drunk too much. I was tired, lonely and still rattled from my encounter with Dr Morales. On an icy cold night when I felt my future falling away like an abyss in front of me, her company was warm and reassuring. I let myself be persuaded that the trip over the mountains would be much less enjoyable without her. Instead of arriving home in disgrace, having failed to earn my degree, I would return to Santa Cruz with Rosalinda on my arm. I knew my parents would be delighted.

Stepping among the clusters of sleeping Indians, we crossed the park and entered the cathedral by a side door. The air was cold, but at least we were out of the wind. The only light came from a nativity scene in a chapel to our right. A crude wooden shed with a thatched roof had been erected, the stone floor had been strewn with hay, and life-sized papier-mâché figures of the holy family set in place. But the animals were real: a cow lay in the hay, peacefully chewing its cud; there was also a llama, some sheep, a donkey and two native pigs – long, hairy creatures. The scene, mysteriously illuminated by a light concealed behind the manger, resembled one of the smoky Indian huts that dotted the countryside around Arequipa. All except the cow; in the Andes cows were unheard of.

'My God!' Rosalinda whispered. 'I'd completely forgotten this thing was still here. I didn't even notice it this morning at the funeral.'

'Listen,' I said. 'I think you should go home before anyone discovers you're gone. I don't want you to get into trouble. I'm certain these guys are on my trail. I don't know what they want, but they know I'm going to Santa Cruz. They probably don't care about me much. They can't figure me out. They don't really understand my connection with Charlie. Maybe they think I'm a servant who's been adopted by the family. They're not too interested in me. The fact that I've got Indian blood must lower my value as a kidnap victim, but they'd grab you in a flash if they had a chance. Why isn't your house guarded by the police day and night?'

'Daddy refused to have them. He put his foot down. Not here. Not at home or at Juanpablo. He wants a few days of freedom before he becomes President.' Rosalinda took my hand. 'Come over here. If anyone does come looking for us, we can bury ourselves in the hay, or hide behind the cow. After all, she's mine. Hello, Bessie.'

We climbed the fence, crept among the animals to the rear of the shed, and lay down.

'How do you like it?'

'It is kind of cosy here,' I had to admit. 'Warm.'

'You see? Bessie and the other animals give off a great deal of heat.'

I stretched out. In another minute I was snoring. Rosalinda covered me with hay. She told me later what happened next.

While I was asleep she reconsidered the facts and concluded that I was right – it was foolhardy to run off at a time when her father needed her. She tried to wake me to tell me she had changed her mind, but I was out like a light. She crawled from the shed and went to the entrance of the cathedral, intending to go home. Putting an ear to the door, she opened it a crack when all of a sudden she heard voices. Darting back to the nativity scene, she fell to her knees by the fence. She was just able to assume an attitude of prayer with her forehead pressed against the wooden rail when the door opened and her father and Cousin Teofilio, Arequipa's Chief of Police, came in. The beam of a flashlight swept the stone floor of the cathedral.

'She's not likely to be in church, Josh, is she? On New Year's Eve? What's the point of coming in here?'

'No, Teo, but we can talk here. I asked you to meet me in the church because I didn't want to wake the family. I'm sorry to have had to telephone you at one-thirty in the morning, and on New Year's Eve, too, but there's nothing to be alarmed about. I'm not worried – not yet. I asked you to come here because, if her disappearance turns out to be more serious than I think it is, you should be informed.'

'I'm at your service, Josh.' Cousin Teofilio clicked his heels together. 'Any time of the day or night, 365 days a year!'

Cousin Teo was known among the Calderón clan as 'The Village Idiot'. He had risen to the exalted position of Chief of Police, not through brain power, of which he was in short supply, but because of his slavish obedience to Charlie, whose ruthlessness he sought to emulate. Once a year on Boxing Day when, according to the family's English tradition, the Calderóns distributed gifts to their servants, Teo and his Honduran wife Viguittar were condescendingly invited to the big house for lunch.

What with his huge shapeless frame, drooping walrus moustache, and slavering desire to please, Teo reminded me of a shaggy Old English sheepdog. The diminutive Viguittar, by comparison, was a terrier.

When I asked Aunt Mary how her name was pronounced, she replied wryly, 'It rhymes with big eater.'

Teo had picked her up in a nightclub in Panama City and brought her back to so-called married respectability in Arequipa. Their only child, a boy, died of leukaemia at the age of ten, after which Viguittar, emptied of whatever human feelings were left within her, devoted herself entirely to the accumulation of material wealth.

In spite of her expensive tastes, she reeked of cheap perfume, a hangover from her days as a call girl. Sometimes her hair was coloured yellow, orange, or a combination of the two. Her front teeth were gold, and the ends of her fingers looked as though they had been dipped in blood.

During lunch, whenever she deigned to rest her eyes on me, I felt an energy of pure hatred flowing across the table. She, who was invited to the big house but once a year, could not understand why a half-breed was welcome to sit down for every Sunday lunch with The Cork.

Boxing Day lunch was the highlight of her social calendar, rivalled in importance only by her annual shopping spree at Bloomingdale's in New York. She was a tireless consumer, and it was put about at the university that she urged Teo to adopt heavy-handed tactics against the *ambulantes* so she could get on with her shopping undisturbed. It was also rumoured that she encouraged her husband to accept bribes to finance her extravagance. Teo's truncheon-wielding riot squads were feared and despised by the students, who said that Viguittar supplied the brains and he the brawn to their sinister relationship. They complemented each other perfectly – a two-headed monster.

'Little more than an hour ago she kissed everyone goodnight and went off to bed,' Uncle Joshua said. 'I was in bed myself, thinking about the future of Peru, thinking about life without Charlie, when suddenly I remembered that today is her birthday. What with the funeral and preparations for Lima, it had completely slipped my mind. What's more, today is her first birthday at home in four years, and I was planning to leave for Juanpablo in the morning. So I got up and wrote her a letter – a birthday greeting. I went into her room to leave it by the bedside. That's when I discovered the maid, in Rosalinda's bed.'

'Do you mean Santusa Izquierda? Did she say where Rosalinda was?' Teofilio asked.

'Santusa's an ignorant, superstitious peasant girl. Rosalinda had told her to get under the covers and stay there until morning. She doesn't know anything.'

'Where do you think she went?'

'I imagine she went to say goodbye to her cousin James.'

'That half-breed adopted nephew of yours?' Teo remarked peevishly. 'He hangs around with a pretty seedy crowd at the university.'

'Don't tell me you're having him watched, too!'

'These days we watch everyone.'

'There's no need to be so suspicious. Not everyone at San Agustín belongs to the Shining Path.'

'If you knew who his friends were, you might not be so keen to have him to Sunday lunch.'

'Teo, I don't think it's your place to tell me who I may or may not invite into my home.'

'Yes, sir.' He clicked his heels again. 'I was only thinking of the security of you and your family. Sorry.'

'He's my brother's adopted son, and I told George we'd look after him. Unfortunately, he missed getting his degree, and he's going back to Santa Cruz in the morning. He was supposed to come by the house this evening to say goodbye to everybody but he didn't turn up. Rosalinda was worried – she's very fond of him. He's a nice boy – a bit insecure . . .'

'With a face like that . . .' Teo laughed, 'what do you expect?'

'Teo, he was tortured as a child. The scars on his face are probably nothing compared to those on his soul. I don't think it's your duty to criticize my nephew.'

'Yes, sir. Sorry.' Click.

'I went to his apartment, but no one was there. He's probably gone out on the town to celebrate, and my guess is that she sneaked out to be with him.'

The lights flashed over the nativity scene and came to rest on the back of Rosalinda, who was pretending to pray by the fence.

'Hello. Josh, there is somebody here.'

Swinging their flashlights, Uncle Joshua and Cousin Teofilio approached and stood by the fence. The steamy breaths of the animals rose in the frigid air.

'She arranged all this before she went fishing with Charlie,' Uncle Joshua said wistfully. 'Practically built this hut with her bare hands . . . she and two of her former team-mates. They collected the animals, and Rosalinda donated that cow from the farm. You should have seen the sensation it created, Teo. The church was full, full – the Indians came from everywhere.'

'And they're still coming, it seems. Hey, you. . . .' The Chief of Police kicked Rosalinda hard in the back with the toe of his shoe. 'It's about time you went home!'

Rosalinda told me later that she bit her tongue to keep from screaming in pain. That viciously delivered kick had landed right on her sacroiliac. She almost fainted, but gripped the rail and stayed on her knees.

'For God's sake, Teo, let him be!' Uncle Joshua remonstrated. 'He probably hasn't got a home to go to.'

'There's not an Indian in this country who doesn't have a home.'

'I hope you're joking. If you are, it's a joke in bad taste.'

'Show me a homeless Indian in Peru. One homeless Indian.'

'Teo, have you gone mad? Have you visited the *barriadas* recently? Those are not homes, they're hovels!'

'And every Indian has his hovel.'

'Which is why the Shining Path has been so successful recruiting in the *barriadas*. Teo, sometimes I think you carry out your duties rather too zealously.'

Rosalinda had covered her face with her hands and was mumbling fervently, cursing her brutal cousin under her breath.

'If you want my opinion, Josh,' Teo said, 'Rosalinda and every member of your family should never leave the house without a bodyguard. Even so, it may be premature to send out an alert. After all, it is New Year's Eve *and* her birthday. *You're* the one who shouldn't be out.'

'It's a sad day for Peru when I can't cross the street to go to church.'

'Better a sad Peru than a dead president-elect. We've learned that the Shining Path is planning a terrorist attack to coincide with your inauguration.'

'What sort of attack?'

'We don't know yet, but you can be sure it'll be something pretty barbaric. Listen, Josh, this business of refusing police protection is very unwise. The Shining Path are closer to you than you think.'

'What exactly do you mean?'

'Santusa Izquierda is not the ignorant, superstitious girl she pretends to be. She was a student at the university and she was recruited by Morales.'

'Not Santusa!'

Rosalinda told me she was absolutely stunned to hear this, and Uncle Joshua sounded shaken by the news, too.

'How long have you known this, Teo?' he asked.

'We've known for some time that Santusa is an informer. We haven't told you because we need to watch her while she watches you. We need to know who she reports to. It's the only way we can break into this elaborate cell structure Dr Morales has constructed. It's like a gigantic termite hill. Once you get inside, there's a thousand different tunnels to choose from. Don't worry, Josh. Santusa is no danger to your family. That's why we let her stay in place.'

Uncle Joshua bowed his head. 'I'm sorry, Teo, but what with Charlie's funeral on top of everything else, it's all been a bit too much for me. And tomorrow I have to say goodbye to Juanpablo, which is the only place I want to be.'

'Does the maid know you're going to Juanpablo?'

'It's not exactly a state secret. Of course she knows. The whole family knows.'

'How are you planning to go there?'

'In the station wagon, like I always do.'

'That's out of the question. It would be too easy for the Shining Path to ambush you. You'll have to make the trip by helicopter.'

'But I've promised the children. . . .'

'Don't worry. After your television appearances during the election, the whole country knows you're a family man and that you never go anywhere without your family. We ordered one especially from Sikorsky to accommodate you and the children. I'm putting it at your disposal tomorrow. I've also taken the liberty of installing a telephone at Juanpablo.'

'Teo, we've never had a phone at Juanpablo!'

'You have now. The President of Peru cannot be cut off from the affairs of state. Now you can pick up the phone and be in direct contact with military headquarters here in Arequipa, or the White House in Washington, DC, for that matter. . . . Sh! What's that noise? Is someone asleep in there?'

For a minute they didn't say anything. Rosalinda held her breath and listened, too. In the silence that followed, she said that my snoring was clearly audible.

'Someone's asleep in there.' Uncle Joshua flashed his light into the interior of the shed. 'Shall we have a look?'

'That's the snore of a drunken Indian.' Cousin Teo looked down at Rosalinda, who was still on her knees. Uncle Joshua must have been gazing at her, too. Had he turned his light on her then, he might have noticed that the heels of her sandalled feet were neither calloused nor cracked, and our fateful journey might never have taken place.

They left the fence and walked to the door of the cathedral.

'You know, Teo, I'm afraid this business of being a president is going to be a terrible ordeal. If you want to know the truth, I'm dreading it. I'm not the man who can tame this country.'

'Don't talk like that, Josh. Remember your loyalties. This country's in a hell of a mess. Some of the top families are already thinking of pulling out. We're in danger of being taken over by Communists and there could be a civil war, not to speak of the kidnappings, the extortion, the terrorism. You're our last hope, Josh. The Shining Path are getting a hold in the provinces. No one's safe, not even in their own homes. Did you know that 600 cars were stolen in Lima last month?'

'My family comes before anything else.'

'The whole country is looking to you to save it.'

'This Shining Path group – do you think we should try to get in touch with them?'

'You don't seem to understand the kind of people we're dealing with, Josh,' Cousin Teofilio groaned, exasperated. 'They're ruthless. They don't just want to overthrow your government, they want to overthrow every government. They want to destroy civilization. You can't talk to them. The only thing you can do is shoot them, or put them in prison. The sooner they're eliminated, the better.'

'These people are human beings, Teo, not some vermin that need to be exterminated.'

'They're killers, Josh, like the PLO, the IRA, the Red Brigades. They want to destroy the existing order. There's nothing heroic or romantic about the Shining Path. That guy Morales is no better than Pol Pot. They do their recruiting with drugs, or at gunpoint.'

'They speak for the aspirations of millions of Peruvians.'

'Indians, you mean.'

'Teo, the Indians are Peruvians just like you and me!' Uncle Joshua said forcefully. 'When their children die, they shed tears, just as you grieved when Carlos died.'

'They contribute next to nothing to the prosperity of this country,' Teo replied, echoing Charlie's view.

'Their contribution is irrelevant. As human beings, they are entitled to life, liberty and the pursuit of happiness. That is going to be the moral foundation of my administration, and any government official who does not give it wholehearted support will be in danger of losing his job! Do you understand, Teo?'

'Yes, sir!' Rosalinda said that Teo's heels were clicking like castanets.

'Have you cried since the day Carlos died?'

'No, I have not.'

'We are surrounded by misery. Have you or Viguittar shed one single tear for the misfortune of others?'

'Since Carlos died, I have no more tears.'

'None?'

'I do my duty.'

'If you ever manage to capture this Dr Morales, Teo, I want you to bring him to me. He is not to be tortured or executed. I want to listen to what he has to say about the future of Peru.'

'I'll tell you exactly what he wants. He wants to rid Peru of foreign influences. By that he means you and me. He's renounced the twentieth century. His group would like to see Peru slip into complete anarchy, so he can install himself as the country's saviour. He'd be just the same as Mao, Ortega, Castro and all those other left-wing dictators. He'd do away with democracy, close down parliament, the newspapers, TV and radio, gag the Church and all his political opponents – starting with you,' he added smugly.

'The Shining Path's actions seem irrational to us, Teo, but in a local context they make some sense. Many of the Indian peasants have never received the slightest benefit from things like electric light, schools, banks, roads or bridges, so they have little compunction in destroying them.'

'He wants to replace Spanish with Quechua as the official language!' Rosalinda said Teo's voice was becoming increasingly strident. 'He wants to raze Lima to the ground and make Cuzco the capital again! He wants to return this country to the Stone-Age Indian republic it was before the Conquest!'

'Calm down, Teo! It's not the end of the world.'

'But I tell you it is – the end of our world!'

'I wish to talk with him. I want to learn how he proposes to achieve all this.'

'We've heard reports that Dr Morales may be hiding out here in Arequipa and planning to take a crack at you or your family even before you take office. If Rosalinda's not back by breakfast time, every police officer in the city will be alerted.'

'Don't be too hasty, Teo. I don't want any false alarms. Rosalinda's not the kind of girl to do something foolish. I'll let you know as soon as she comes in.'

'Josh,' Teo said meekly, 'Viguittar and I want to offer you and your family our deepest condolences . . . there were too many people at the funeral, and we didn't get a chance. Charlie was a great man. . . .'

Uncle Joshua was silent for a minute. 'Not a great man, Teo, but a successful one.'

'Not a great man?' Cousin Teo sounded flabbergasted.

'He lacked humanity. He got the job done, but he did it without compassion. The same goes for you, Teo. If you want to keep your job, from now on do it with compassion. And I think you should tell Viguittar that, as long as I am President, she will have to curtail her spending.'

'Yes, sir.' Click.

As soon as they had left the cathedral, Rosalinda got to her feet and ran to the door and looked out. Then she returned to the shed and again tried to wake me up, but I was still dead to the world. She lay down in the hay but did not sleep. She decided to carry out her plan to come with me after all. That her father and her cousin, standing three feet away, had been completely taken in by her disguise excited her far too much to go home again. Her back was killing her, but she was too kindled by the spirit of adventure to feel much pain. Her father, she realized, was not unduly worried about her absence. Moreover, he would find her letter by his breakfast plate in the morning, and everything would be explained.

11

The train was scheduled to depart at seven. At one minute to the hour, it was standing peacefully in the station. The ancient steam locomotive, which ought to have been in a museum, sighed and from time to time emitted diminutive plumes of vapour. The passengers milled about the platform chatting with well-wishers, fondling babies, making last-minute purchases, and weighing bundles on a large pair of scales.

PRICE OF CARGOES		
Tomatoes the crate	500
Eggs the box	500
Potatoes the sack	500
Wire the roll	500

Indian women, crowding beneath the windows of the train, held up their goods and cried out in thin, plaintive voices: 'Ice cream! Cheese! Bread! Sandwiches! What do you desire, sir?'

No one seemed to notice the stationmaster who stepped smartly from his office. Marching briskly forward with the determined air of a drill sergeant, he cleaved the passive crowd and arrived at the head of the train, where he executed an abrupt about-face. For a few seconds he stood to attention before blowing sharply on a brass horn. The train began to move.

The result was panic. Conversations were cut short, babies were practically thrown away, and people who had been idly haggling over the price of a single tortilla pulled out wads of money, seized the tortillas by the handful and ran for the train.

With passengers still piling on board and hanging on for dear life, we steamed out of Arequipa. The stationmaster was still standing to attention at the end of the platform, viewing the pandemonium with an expression of grim satisfaction on his face.

Rosalinda told me about the conversation between Uncle Joshua and Teofilio in the church. 'Daddy must have found my letter by now,' she said hopefully. 'Otherwise the station would have been crawling with police, don't you think?'

'I don't know what to think. I just hope you know what you're doing. This business of Santusa being connected with the Shining Path scares me, but if he got your letter and knows you're with me, and he's not worried, then I guess it's all right.'

'I was so proud of Daddy standing up to that insensitive brute. I'm going to tell him that Teofilio ought to be fired.'

'Just show him that bruise on your back. Teo won't last another minute in his job.'

After passing a vast necropolis on the left, the train, with much hooting and screeching, climbed through the shadowy columns of a eucalyptus forest above the city. Sunlight flickered through the peeling, festooned branches.

Rosalinda was hanging out the window and calling, 'Goodbye, Charlie! Goodbye!' She fell back into her seat and smiled through the tears. 'We never spoke much, you know. It was just, "Cast your line here", or, "Don't let your shadow fall on the water." A few minutes before he drowned, we had tea on his rock, and we didn't say anything at all. I loved that silence, the feeling of not having to speak. When I pulled him out of the water, his body was already stiff, like a kitten I had once that died.'

Down the aisle an American woman in a grey business suit was making a fuss over her baggage, which consisted to our surprise of two truck tyres. The conductor was protesting because they blocked the aisle. He wanted her to roll them into the baggage car and even volunteered to help her do it, but the woman was roosting on the tyres like a mother hen. She crossed her arms over her chest and refused to budge. The conductor continued to harangue her, but the woman had ceased to pay attention. Out of the corner of her eye she was furtively scrutinizing Rosalinda, who had fallen asleep in the seat next to me.

I looked down at her. She had even taken the trouble to rouge her face to simulate the chapped cheeks of a mountain youth. The authenticity of her disguise notwithstanding, in broad daylight she looked less like an Indian boy and more like a Spanish girl.

The train, meanwhile, was skirting some low hills. Llamas were standing on the watery plain. Their images were reflected in the rain puddles. The shadow-patched plain was bright green but faded to blue in the distance. The snow-capped peaks stood all about. This was the Altiplano, and we were headed for the green centre of the continent. There were sheep out there, and a surprising abundance of green grass. Tiny figures in the distance were waving at the train. Indians toting huge loads held in place by head slings shuffled off across a plain that swept up into the clouds like a highway to eternity.

The grass gave way before a desert of white sand. The sand turned out to be the shore of a shrinking lake. As the train surged along a causeway dividing the broad shallow body of water, thousands of flamingos took flight. The train whistle chased coots, ducks, cormorants, seagulls and herons into the air. Fearing metal, they flew off across the vast gloomy lake. They were heading home to the marshes, to the safety of the reed beds.

Having traversed the plain, the train began to climb. The bleak and blasted mining communities at eleven, twelve, thirteen thousand feet looked like the last towns on earth, which one day they might well be. After the bombs have fallen, that is, and the rest of the world's population has been wiped out.

Everywhere the same message had been scrawled on rocks in the mountains and on the walls of mud houses:

El Pueblo Muere de Hambre
Pan Para Todo

Lives and faces appeared as monochromatic as the russet ore scraped from the earth and hauled by the old, old, unbelievably old but still serviceable steam locomotives. At each stop, Indian women the shape and resilience of rubber balls besieged the train.

'Cheese! What do you desire, sir?'

This was the land of llamas and bowler hats, appropriate to Indian formality. Yet they still played soccer at these altitudes. It was getting colder and colder, and snowfields lay all about. The wind whipped dust from the players' feet. The train sped onwards, scattering the llamas grazing beside the track. When it stopped, the villagers scrambled for newspapers. They were starved of news, too. Half the population of these oriental Tibetan-like communities was composed of ambulatory vendors who boarded the train, even before it came to a complete halt, by the dozen or by the hundred.

'Bread! What do you desire, sir? For God's sake, have pity! Tell me what you desire.'

By mid-morning the pass was reached. It was snowing. A large number of Indians had gathered about the train, but their pitiful cries were muffled by falling snow. The vendors competed for pennies, but the bitter cold muted their repeated supplications. A pistol-packing teenage soldier came on board. He patrolled the aisle with an exaggerated, self-conscious swagger. It didn't work because he was too skinny. The huge revolver on his hip looked theatrical. He was shivering, too, so nobody paid any attention to him.

Outside, a group of Indian boys was standing next to a sign. Against the gloomy, shadowless background (all the surrounding peaks had been obscured by falling snow), they hopefully held up strings of mountain trout.

4,447 METRES ABOVE THE LEVEL OF THE SEA

Rosalinda woke up and spotted the fish. 'Look at those trout,' she exclaimed. 'I'm starved!'

Tyre-lady, with whom I had already exchanged some friendly glances, came down the aisle. She had curly grey hair cut short like a man's. Bright blue eyes gave her an alert, intelligent expression. She looked about fifty-five or sixty.

'Excuse me for butting in,' she said with almost exaggerated politeness, 'but I couldn't help overhearing you speaking English. Would you and your wife like to eat those trout for lunch?'

'My wife?' I looked at Rosalinda. 'Ah . . . '

'I love trout,' Rosalinda piped up. Everybody on the train had been waiting for her to wake. Now they were all staring at her. The Indian women stopped chewing their pumpkin seeds and gaped.

'So do I,' I said.

'Particularly fried trout,' Rosalinda added. 'That's the way Charlie liked them.'

I wiped the moisture from the window with the tip of my finger and looked outside. 'How're we going to cook them?'

'Don't worry about a thing.' The woman jutted out her chin and stood up a little straighter, as though such a trivial consideration only stiffened her resolve. 'I'll take care of everything.'

She marched off.

'Trout for breakfast!' Rosalinda was gazing appreciatively at the woman's truck tyres. 'She's awfully friendly.'

'She's been watching you all morning,' I said. 'I think she's got a crush on you.'

'Look at those gorgeous truck tyres and look at those trout.' Rosalinda had tucked her feet beneath her and was acknowledging the smiles of the Indian women who were nodding in approval at her boyish costume. 'God, I could eat them raw!'

Through the window the woman could be seen talking with the Indian boys. They gathered eagerly about her; they wanted to sell her the whole lot. It had begun to snow much harder – a swirling blast of wet, heavy flakes. It looked as though the price of fish was going to come way, way down. Before the deal was concluded, the storm engulfed them; they were lost from sight in the snow.

What I saw out there almost made me jump out of my seat. Two Indians were standing by the tracks.

'Get down!' I said to Rosalinda. 'Get away from the window!'

'Why? What's wrong?'

'Your friends are out there!'

'What friends? Who?'

'Sinesio and . . . '

'And Amador? Where?'

I was in a cold sweat. 'Stay down! Don't look!'

'Why? What's wrong?'

We ducked down from the window.

'I don't want them to see you.'

'Why not?'

'Nobody should know you're on this train. They may be spying out for the Shining Path.'

'I don't believe that.'

'You didn't suspect Santusa, either. Even if they're not, if they told the wrong person that they saw you on the train, we could be in trouble. It's too much of a coincidence that they're here.'

Now Rosalinda was nervous. 'Do you think they saw us?'

'I don't know. It's snowing hard. There's a lot of condensation on the window.'

The inside of my throat contracted, as though someone were trying to choke me. Filled with a sense of impending doom, I slid from my seat and pulled Rosalinda down with me. My heart was pounding. In the jungle I knew how to hide myself, but where was safety here?

The train had begun to move. We looked out. Indian women ran alongside, frantically waving their goods. Prices were dropping towards zero. The fish boys were dividing up the money and had already begun to fight. A snowball spattered against the window. There was a rock inside it that

75

cracked the glass.

The woman was standing before us, triumphantly holding up a string of green trout. Her curly hair and eyebrows were frosted with snow.

I reached for my wallet.

'Please, sir.' She grabbed my hand and pulled me to my feet. 'It's my pleasure.'

'Uh, ma'am.' I could hardly stand. My knees were weak. 'How're you going to cook them?'

'The chef is a friend of mine,' she whispered. 'Follow me, and please call me Dot.'

'Chef?' Rosalinda exclaimed.

'Let's get out of here,' I said.

We dropped our wads of goat cheese and pumpkin seeds and hurried after her.

The train descended quickly and effortlessly through the rock-strewn, pitted canyons. There was no more sound of the locomotive straining; the engineer had put her into neutral and was letting her glide. The tracks twisted crazily, but the curves had been ingeniously banked. Aunt Mary's grandfather had built this railroad, and it was like being on a rollercoaster. Ahead lay the great riverine plain, but first the fine dust entered, kicked up by the gathering speed of the train. The Indians began to cough. Some had brought along canteens.

I was following Dot and Rosalinda through the rattling coaches, when I came face to face with The Armadillo. Still wrapped in his filthy raincoat, he sat with his legs spread apart and his head thrown back. His antique face was distorted by sleep. His mouth was open and he was snoring as his head bumped against the glass.

I crept past and caught up with Rosalinda in between cars. 'Listen!' I grabbed her arm. 'That guy who was shadowing me last night – I just saw him!'

'Where?'

'Don't look back. Keep on going. He was asleep. I don't think he saw us. But this is no coincidence – he's still on my trail!'

'What does he want?'

'I don't know. I haven't the faintest idea. Maybe he doesn't either. He takes his orders from Dr Morales.'

'They had you locked inside that cantina in Arequipa. Why did they let you go?'

'How would I know? Probably they think that because my name is Calderón I have a lot of money. If they knew how much money that Toyota dealership was bringing in, they wouldn't be wasting their time. . . . It's me they're interested in now, Rosalinda, but if he finds out who *you* are, they'll be after you for sure. Do you understand what a prize you would be for the Shining Path? God, I hope your disguise has fooled him so far.'

'Well, they won't get a penny out of Daddy – he still owes thousands to the bank.'

'Don't be so naïve! You've been away too long. Have you forgotten what it means to people in this country that you're Charlie's granddaughter? They think the Calderón family is sitting on all the gold in Peru. And you keep forgetting that your father is going to be President. If they grabbed you, it wouldn't just be a personal tragedy or a family affair, it would be a national disaster. There would be no limit to the ransom they could ask. If they killed you, there'd be an orgy of reprisals. Your father would never take office. The colonels would stay where they are. Democracy would go down the drain in Peru, and there would probably be a civil war.'

'What shall we do?'

'You've got to stay out of sight – lock yourself in the toilet, perhaps.'

'I'd rather jump off the train.'

We looked out at the desolate landscape of salt lakes and extinct volcanoes.

'We wouldn't stand a chance out there. Look – maybe it'll be safer in here.'

Dot had opened the door to the caboose and was beckoning us forward. She woke up a rotund Indian boy by the name of Eustaquio, who was dozing by a pot-belly stove. Eustaquio was all business. He grabbed the trout and gutted them. In no time there was a pot of potatoes on the boil, and the trout were simmering side by side in a big, greasy skillet.

'He helped me this morning in the station.' Dot smiled at Eustaquio. 'Try pushing two big truck tyres along. One is easy, but two together have minds of their own. They insist on rolling in different directions.'

12

'God, I love to eat!' Rosalinda contemplated the morsel of fried trout on the end of her fork before putting it in her mouth. During lunch she had regaled us with stories about her boarding school in England. Dot had slapped her knee and shrieked with laughter as though she were drunk.

Every few minutes I went to the door of the caboose and looked out, but there was no sign of The Armadillo. I felt safer inside. There were four of us now, and a heavy lock on the door. If we could get to Juliaca with its big military camp, I thought, we might be all right.

'I wish I had a daughter like you,' Dot exclaimed. 'God blessed me with a healthy son, so I have nothing to complain about, but you do get tired of buying baseball bats and football shoes and not one frilly thing.'

Dot told us that she had once lived in Peru when her husband, a mining engineer, had been working for Cerro de Pasco. Now she was returning to visit her son, Johnny, a Peace Corps volunteer in Cuzco.

'Thad died last year. He was sixty-two years old and in his prime. Never sick a day in his life. Oh, I wish I could have had ten more years with him.' She sighed and looked out the window. 'November 10th, less than two months ago – it was a Saturday afternoon. I left him in front of the television watching the football game and went to the A & P. I returned an hour later. When I came into the house, I knew something was wrong. When he hears the door shut, Thad always shouts, "That you, Dot?" As if it could be anyone else. I thought, well, it's half-time, and he's raking leaves in the garden. But the TV was still on. I went into the living room, and there he was on the floor. Stone dead.' She went on, speaking more to herself than to us, 'When a man dies, he doesn't keel over like a tree. He crumples into a little pile. Heart attack. Bam. The doctor said he never knew what hit him. Sometimes life creeps up behind you and stabs you in the back when you least expect it. One afternoon I was out buying dinner for the man I had loved my whole life, and an hour later I was all alone with no husband. The house was too big. There was no one to cook for, no one to talk to, no one to dress for – just me and the cat. My friends felt sorry for me. A widow's life, you know, the fun is over. They said I should get out of St Louis for a while, get out of my rut and travel. So I thought, I'll visit Johnny. The Peace Corps frowns on parents visiting the volunteers, but I thought, they can't stop me. Johnny was born here. He loves Peru. What harm can it do?'

Johnny, Dot told us, drove a bookmobile for the Peace Corps's literacy programme. He travelled all over the Andes in his truck, distributing books, setting up rural libraries, and alphabetizing the Indians. He'd covered so many miles that his tyres were getting bald. Mudslides made the mountain roads dangerous. Johnny had been caught in a blizzard once, and nearly froze to death. Now roving bands of terrorists were stopping motorists, demanding money and sometimes killing them.

'Last month Johnny wrote that the Shining Path blew up the train to Machu Picchu and a tourist was killed. He said it's getting to be like Vietnam around here! If it's anything like Vietnam, I told him, it's time the Peace Corps pulled out of Peru. I'm here to find out just how dangerous the situation is. Before coming I wrote him asking what he needed from America. You know, a jar of peanut butter or a new shirt. Two new truck tyres was what he asked for! The ones made here are no good. I'd never bought a tyre in my life, not even a car tyre. I went to Walmart, got these Firestones, and brought them all the way from St Louis. That's why I'm guarding them with my life. Some of the communes where he takes his books are so far off the beaten path that the people have never seen a white man before.'

'He must be very brave,' Rosalinda said.

'Not Shining Path communes, I hope,' I said.

'Johnny wouldn't want to have anything to do with terrorists. After all the killing he saw in Vietnam, he swore he'd never touch a gun again. He joined the Peace Corps because he wants to help people improve their lives and make their future better than the past.'

'That's what the Shining Path preach, too,' I said. 'But they're armed to the teeth and kill anyone who opposes them.'

The dark stream that paralleled the tracks, meanwhile, was growing clearer, the air by perceptible degrees warmer. The train came out under blue sky, into a land of red rocks. The mountains had flattened to hills, the riverbed had widened to half a mile, a grey artery of pebbles.

'I know how to drive a truck,' Rosalinda was telling Dot. 'We have an old apple-green Ford pick-up that Daddy bought second hand from the Ministry of Agriculture. The gears are so stiff that only Manuel our foreman can shift them, and we call him "The Crusher" because his hands are so strong. He taught me. Really, I don't think I've ever done anything that impressed Daddy more than when I got behind the wheel and drove off in the truck.'

'Johnny wrote me a while back that he wished he had a girl to be his assistant driver. I'm sure he'd take you on,' Dot said. 'Girls are more reliable than men, he said. They don't drink. They stand up to cold and fatigue better. They don't drive fast to show off. They don't trade in drugs or smoke dope.'

'I don't know what I'm going to do with my life yet. I like sports, but I've got bosoms now, and I can't run like I used to. I wanted to be a nun, but my grandfather wouldn't hear of it. Daddy wants me to complete my education, so I've applied to go to Harvard next autumn. Even so, he'll be pleased when I tell him you've offered me a job. What I really want is to dedicate my life – not just dedicate, but sacrifice it to some worthy cause – something that'll help my country solve its problems. I'd like to help Daddy stop the Shining Path, bring all the people together, make a great government, and heal Peru. He needs help, because there are so many divisions, and everything is in such a mess. Right now I'm feeling a little guilty because I shouldn't be on this trip. I should be home, by his side, helping him.'

'Is your father in government?' Dot asked, intrigued.

Rosalinda glanced at me. 'He's really a farmer.'

'Ghost Riders in the Sky' blared from Eustaquio's radio. Sullen, bearded gauchos stood by their wattle huts and watched the train go by. Their half-wild, melancholy cows crashed headlong into the bush to escape the train. The narrow-gauge tracks trailed away behind the caboose. They seemed so incongruously correct within the wilderness, so shiny in a dull world; how mysteriously they conducted themselves across the prairie!

Rosalinda crossed herself. It was a bit spooky out there, where the great yellow rivers, like jaundiced serpents, fed off the land. Every living thing owned spikes – spurs, burrs, horns, thorns, beaks, claws, talons. Every dead tree contained a predator. Now there was an invasion of yellow butterflies. They went for the cattle droppings: those turds, golden with a myriad of glittering wings, actually looked as though they might take off. In places where the half-wild Brahmins had been feeding, the butterflies blanketed the turds like shimmering yellow snow agitating for a return to the heavens.

Two bulls had fought by a waterhole. The stricken loser lay stretched upon the ground while the victor stood on shaky legs, keeping at bay the hundreds of vultures that had assembled.

Bang! The train hit a magnificent bull and sent him sprawling in an explosion of dust. A roar went up from the passengers as the engineer slammed on the brakes. People were rushing to the doors and piling out the windows even before the train had stopped. Everyone brandished long knives that had been concealed before. The blades were flashing in the sunlight as the mob charged the bull. The poor animal wasn't even dead yet. He was kicking the dust and trying to get back on his feet. He was a monster; he must have weighed at least a ton. Right beneath our window the mob descended on him and began to cut him up even before he had breathed his last. They slashed his tendons and sunk their knives into his throat.

His arteries spurted crimson. The butchers were dancing in it, like kids under a sprinkler. In a few minutes he was reduced to a bloody mess, and the passengers were reboarding the train lugging hunks of meat the size of suitcases. They were laughing and comparing notes to see who had got the biggest piece. The engineer was out there, too, demanding his share. In Peru, everyone is an amateur butcher. They were singing and wiping their blades clean. Even before the train had started up again, the flies had come aboard.

Rosalinda retreated from the window and crumpled against the wall of the caboose; she would not raise her head until the train had begun to move.

Dot tried to comfort her. 'It's awful, dearie, I know, but the bull was hit hard.'

'He probably wouldn't have survived,' I said.

'It's not the bull I'm worried about – it's Daddy. He'll never be able to manage this country,' she said through her tears. 'He's a father and a farmer, not a man to supervise a slaughter. It was a terrible mistake to have stood in the election. In England I prayed that he wouldn't win. He's too generous and too fair to be President. Now I see why the colonels are always taking over. The only way to control starving people is with a gun. I'm scared, James. This pipe dream of turning Peru into a garden, of reviving Inca agriculture – maybe Charlie could have done it, but Charlie was as tough as nails. People hated him, but he survived and succeeded. Daddy is too gentle. The first crisis will probably kill him. During the Peasant Revolution he simply couldn't cope. He may speak Quechua like an Indian, but when those people invaded the farm, he was speechless. He loves this country too much to govern it. Believe me, I know – I can always pull the wool over his eyes because he loves me so much. You watch, he'll drop the affairs of state and come running to my bedside the first time I have a case of the sniffles. He's too vulnerable. Oh, James, I'm so afraid he'll fall into the first trap.'

Dot was mesmerized. 'Is your father Joshua Calderón, the new President?'

'I'm afraid so.'

Dot gasped with astonishment. 'Johnny says he's the one man who stands between Peru and civil war. If he fails, the whole country will go down with him. He would have voted for him if he could. He thinks he's wonderful, and a very courageous man.'

'We all do,' I said.

'Are you his son-in-law?' asked Dot, turning her attention to me.

'Uh, no, I'm Rosalinda's cousin. Not her real cousin, her – uh, adopted, half-breed, Indian cousin.'

'My favourite cousin and our family conscience.' Rosalinda stood up and put her arm around me. 'He's taking me back to the jungle where he came from.'

'It's her birthday today,' I said.

'Goodness! How old are you?'

'I'm eighteen.'

'Well, I declare. We'll have to make a cake.'

PART

II

13

The train hadn't gone more than a few miles before it stopped again.

Dot poked her head out the window. 'Soldiers,' she said.

'Eustaquio, will you go up to the front of the train and see what's going on?' Rosalinda asked.

After a few minutes he came running back. 'The tracks have been blown up!'

'Who did it?'

'Bandits!'

'Oh my heavens!' Dot cried.

'They were going to rob the train,' he added breathlessly, 'but the soldiers came and chased them away.'

'Oh dear, now the train will be late. Johnny's going to be worried.' Dot subsided into a chair. 'He's waiting for me in Juliaca.'

'Well, it couldn't have happened at a better place.' Rosalinda was pointing out the window. 'Look where we are. We're at Lagunas Lagunillas. Charlie used to come here to fish. That must be the Reina Victoria.'

We peered out the window at an old grey rambling hotel that sat on the plain like a stranded battleship.

'The train is going to spend the night here while the tracks are repaired,' Eustaquio said.

'The lakes around here are full of fish, Dot.' Rosalinda was trying to sound a hopeful note. 'My grandfather said the fishing is better here than in Lake Titicaca.'

'Well, I must make sure my tyres are safe.' With a sigh of resignation Dot stood up. 'Come along, Eustaquio.'

Rosalinda and I got down from the train and walked forward to inspect the damage. A crowd of Indians was standing around the engine, staring impassively at where the earth had been blackened by an explosion. One of the rails was pointing at the sky like an angry, twisted finger.

'I don't know why they bothered to blow up the tracks,' Rosalinda was saying, 'since the train stops here anyway. And if they wanted to rob the train, they must have known there's no one on it with more than five cents in his pocket.'

'The Shining Path stole some cases of dynamite from a gold mine near Putilla last month,' I said.

'That still doesn't explain it, does it? If the Shining Path is trying to promote a Robin Hood image, stealing from the rich and giving to the poor, why would they prey on these Indians?'

'I don't know why they did it,' I told her, but in my heart I thought I did know. The Shining Path had blown up the tracks because they were planning to kidnap me.

An army truck with a long antenna waving from the cab was pulled up by the tracks. Two soldiers with kalashnikovs were standing beside it, and they were talking to The Armadillo. I ducked behind the Indians and yanked Rosalinda down with me.

'What's wrong, James? What are you doing?'

'That's him!'

'Who?'

'The one I was telling you about. The one with the soldiers,' I whispered. 'I don't want him to see me!'

'Shall I look?'

'No. All right – you look. But don't let them see you! What's he doing?'

She slowly raised her head up. 'The soldiers have him. . . . They're talking to him. . . . They're putting him in the truck.'

'Good. I hope it means they've arrested him.'

'Shouldn't you tell the soldiers he was following you?'

'No! Let them handle it. They've got him – that's the main thing.'

'I don't see any sign of Sinesio or Amador.'

'Good. Let's hope they aren't on the train.'

The Indian men went and squatted behind the cactus trees. Their women collected firewood. They were going to roast the meat and sleep by the tracks. Attracted by the smell of raw meat, a number of pariah dogs skulked about. Anyone with more than five cents in his pocket headed for the hotel.

That was us. We trailed through the cactus trees, Dot whistling as she led the way. For her, this was Miami beach. Each footstep caused an eruption of dust. Heat-shrouded volcanoes shimmered in the distance and the metallic sky was low and flat, like the bottom of a tin plate.

'This is an unexpected bonus,' Rosalinda said. 'I feel I should go fishing here in memory of Charlie. Will you come with me, James?'

'All right.'

In a depression near the hotel, a kind of circular crater that could have been ploughed up by a meteor, we came upon a patched-up old circus tent.

'Good Lord.' Rosalinda stood there with her feet planted. 'Are we in Africa?' She pointed at a rather gaunt elephant which had just padded around the side of the tent, followed by a man wearing a green jacket. When it saw us, the elephant broke into a shuffling trot. It looked as though it was trying to escape its keeper, but it stopped at a place where the dust was deep. It sucked up a trunkful and snorted it over its back.

'This is her greatest pleasure!' the keeper shouted at us from the pit. 'I should say her *only* pleasure!'

'What's an elephant doing here?' Rosalinda asked.

'We used to belong to a circus,' the man said. He was a short man with a hatchet face. Beneath a narrow, wrinkled brow two little eyes sat side by side. A long nose sloped downwards and off to the left, as though it were made of wax and had melted.

'Los Hermanos Gallo from Rosario. We played in Asunción, Concepción and Corumba. It was a very fine circus. *Muy bueno*. There were midgets and freaks, acrobats and clowns. We had a plastic man and gauchos cracking whips. But the greatest attraction of all was this elephant. We played in Santa Cruz and Cochabamba, La Paz and Puno, and everyone came to see this elephant. We were on our way to Arequipa and Lima, but when the train came here, the engineer said, "This animal is too heavy. My motor will not pull it over the mountains. We will all die in the snow." So we got down here. That was four years ago,' he concluded on a note of resignation and self-pity. 'The circus never came back to us.'

'That must be the elephantless circus that Charlie took the children to when I was in England,' Rosalinda whispered. 'And this must be the missing elephant.'

The elephant let out a hoot.

'You'll have to excuse her,' the keeper said. 'She doesn't ordinarily behave like this. Do you, Nuria?' With his stick he scratched the elephant behind the ear. 'It's that bomb that went off this morning. Pow! Scared us out of our wits. Nuria is still upset. Aren't you, dear?'

The elephant let out a little moan and gave the man an affectionate goose with the tip of its trunk.

'Hey!' The narrow, unhappy face broke into a freakish smile.

'Did you see the ones who did it?' I asked.

'Heck no. You know what bombs mean in Peru – Shining Path. I kept my head down and stayed in the tent to comfort Nuria. She was shaking all over. Elephants are sensitive creatures, you know. They don't like loud noises. You folks coming to the show tonight?'

We looked at each other. 'What show?'

'Nuria will be performing at eight o'clock. Can't you see how excited she is? You'll be our first audience in a month.'

'Is Nuria getting enough *salt*?' Rosalinda asked.

The elephant, which had been rolling contentedly in the dust, suddenly let out a terrific trumpet blast. She struggled to her feet. She was flapping her ears and waving her trunk. It was all the keeper could do to control her with his stick.

We hurried on to the hotel.

14

The Reina Victoria loomed ahead. The land between the hotel and the railroad tracks had been eroded into ravines and gullies, with narrow paths winding along the ridges. A flat area in front of the hotel had been made into a soccer pitch. Twin piles of whitewashed stones marked the goalposts.

At the entrance to the hotel we paused beneath a sign.

> COLONEL FAWCETT SLEPT HERE
> On February 12, 1905 the famous Amazonian explorer slept here after having walked out of the wilderness of the Beni where he had been missing and presumed eaten by the dreaded Wayana.

'That's my tribe,' I said.

'Are you descended from cannibals?' Dot asked.

'Cannibals and missionaries,' I replied. 'The worst of both worlds.'

'It just goes to show – doesn't it?' Rosalinda said. 'Charlie always said that in Peru the Stone Age isn't thousands of years in the past, it's right back there around the corner.'

'And who knows?' I replied. 'The way things are going, it could be that it's right around the next corner, too.'

'Well, if it is,' Dot said, 'I want my boy to be safe home in St Louis, Missouri.'

'Charlie told me the hotel was built during the rubber boom. It was popular with fishermen who came to fish for the huge trout in the lakes. But recently the tourists have been scared off by the Shining Path.'

'Well, let's hope the soldiers have chased them away from

round here.'

The exterior of the hotel had been bleached by the sun and scoured by flying sand. It was the colour of driftwood. The interior, however, was clean, dark and cool. The hardwood floors from the forest had been oiled and polished. The chairs and sofas were leather and the tables were mahogany. Skins of jaguar and ocelot decorated the walls of the lobby, along with numerous stuffed fish. The wall above the reception desk was hung with posters of the great hotels of the world – the Hermitage in Monte Carlo, the Palace in St Moritz, the Ritz in Madrid, and the Touristas in Tingo Maria. A glass case contained a row of grinning, trepanned skulls that dated from pre-Columbian days. In the centre of the room stood a soccer table.

'We'd like some rooms for tonight.' Dot was talking to a trio of ancient Indians in starched khaki uniforms who stood in a row behind the desk.

'Any one you like, missus,' one of them replied. 'Every room is free.'

'Are you going to come fishing with us, Dot?' Rosalinda asked.

'You go ahead, dearie. I've had enough fish for one day. I'm going to put my feet up. Wrestling with those tyres wore me out.'

'Wait for me, James, will you?' Rosalinda said. 'I'm going up to change out of these clothes.'

'Sure.'

While they were upstairs I examined a framed, bigger than life-sized, official photo of Colonel Anastasio Bustamente y Bilbao, leader of the departing junta, that hung above the door. This *de facto* President of Peru was decked out in white tie and tails, with medals adorning his chest and a crimson sash running diagonally across it. Heavy-jowled and overweight, he seemed to be sneering at his country with a kind of weary disdain. It was an expression of mingled arrogance and dismay, which probably reflected his attitude towards Peru, espccially the Indian population. Perhaps it would be with this same expression, I thought, that he might greet, one

92

night upon returning from some state banquet, the assassins who would await him. His eyebrows were slightly arched in surprise. The photo was taken by flash, and I could imagine him turning on the light, his eyes unaccustomed to the sudden glare, confronting a death squad from the Shining Path.

And what about Uncle Joshua? I wondered. Would he meet the same fate?

'Here I am!' Rosalinda bounced down the stairs.

And here she was, with her black hair just brushed so it floated like a gauzy mane about her shoulders. She had put on her English outfit that she had brought along in her basket – tweed jacket and skirt, knee socks and tasselled walking shoes. The sturdy cloth contrasted with the floppy collar of her creamy silk blouse so that her mannish costume made her seem, if anything, even more feminine. What with her English connections, a degree from Harvard, and her father President, she was undoubtedly destined for great things: Ambassador to Washington, perhaps, or to the Court of St James; while I pursued an illustrious career selling jeeps in Bolivia.

'Well, are you ready?'

'Have you read this?' I was standing in front of a bulletin board with tourist information tacked to it.

VISIT THE RUINS OF ALTAR SACRIFICIO

where, at the precise moment of sunset, the Incan priests once conducted human sacrifices in the belief that blood must be spilled for the wheel of life to move forward.

Peru is a very ancient country. All who sojourn here are, or soon will become, deeply impressed by the mystic atmosphere hanging over this strange land where the Inca religion continues to this day. There may, and probably does, still remain in some Quechua dream, the subconscious perception of the cyclic notions of the antique world: that what has been will come again. When the wheel of life comes full circle, and the life-forces rise in an ascending arc, ancient glories will be restored and men will take up again the ancient parts that were once played by others they never knew, not even in the most shadowy ghost of a dead

93

tradition. There may be, and probably still is, in some remote Andean village, a lone man who to this day guards the secret of untold millions. *¿Quien sabe?*

– Courtesy of 'Friends of the Andes', the Puno Province Archaeological and Historical Society.

A path led among the blossoming cactus trees. The cactus flowers seemed incongruously bright and fragile atop the enormous dull-green growths. These cactus trees looked as though they had been reared from the bottom of the sea on antediluvian roots upon which the sun had never shone.

We came to the lake. Rosalinda stood by the edge and looked across the water for a long time without speaking. At an immense altitude condors soared. She was frowning.

'What's wrong?' I asked.

'This lake – this is the lake where Charlie drowned. In my dream, I mean. He must have described it to me. That's why I dreamed about it. I couldn't possibly have imagined it, could I? It's incredible – isn't it? This lake which I've never seen before is exactly like the lake in my dream.'

'It's kind of spooky if you ask me,' I said. 'I don't like lakes. They make me think of death. It's said that water dreams are all about oblivion and death.'

'It does look frozen, doesn't it?'

It was true. Not a breath of air stirred; the surface of the lake was as smooth as glass, or ice.

A reed canoe was drawn up on the shore. A pole lay across it.

'Let's borrow it,' Rosalinda said. 'It's too shallow to fish from the shore.'

I pushed off, and soon we were gliding across the mirrored surface of the lake. Rubbing each metal joint against the side of her nose, Rosalinda put together her fly rod which, like everything else, came from England. She showed me her collection of flies, which she had made herself.

'Charlie taught me,' she said. 'When I was about ten years old I found a hundred *sole* note in a ditch on the way home from school. You can't buy a sack of potatoes with it now, what with the inflation, but in those days it was worth quite a lot of money, you know, about five dollars. To me it seemed a fantastic sum and it took me ages to decide what I was going to do with it. Finally I made up my mind. Charlie took me to the tackle shop, and I bought a fly-tying kit. There was a little vice to hold the hook, with a magnifying glass to look through, and an assortment of feathers and hairs and threads and hooks. Charlie showed me how to do it. After a few failures, I finally came up with one he said he'd try. On the very first cast, he got a strike!'

Rosalinda wiped away a tear and tied on a fly. 'I always start with Brown Spider,' she said, biting off the leader, 'before moving on to the brighter ones. Like cheeses, you taste the bland one first. . . . ' She started flicking the rod back and forth, and paying out the line from the ticking reel. 'In England I took fly-fishing lessons from an old man called Dan. He lived by the Spey River in Scotland. He taught me the Spey cast . . . like this.' The line snapped out like a whip. She took a short cast back and to the right. Then she flipped the fly forward, rolling her wrist from right to left. 'It comes in handy when there's brush or trees behind. The line must land first, then leader, then fly. Maybe I should have brought sinking line, too. Dan always signed his letters "Tight lines". That was his motto. . . . Here, want to give it a try?'

I took the rod from her. We felt a breeze in our faces. The sun made a brief appearance.

'I bought it for six pounds in Oxford. I love it. It's light. Why pay more? Cast over there. . . . It's too weedy here. . . . That's it.'

The boat drifted with the breeze. Rosalinda took off Brown Spider and tied on a red one.

'We're moving on to Roquefort. Pull the line in in little tugs. That's it. Play the fly.'

A bite! A fish jumped.

'Darn! Lost it.'

'I've been talking too much . . . distracting your attention.'

Another bite!

'Lost him again.'

'Don't pull. Let him swallow it. Remember – tight lines! The magic hour may be approaching. You're doing fine, James. Brilliant technique.'

'We haven't got a net. How are we going to land it?'

'Just drag him in.'

'It wasn't a strong bite. He's not very big. I bet he's not over six inches.'

'Where there are little ones there are big ones. Next time let him swallow it.'

But there wasn't to be a next time. The fish went away, or lost interest. I handed the rod back to Rosalinda.

'The breeze is perfect, isn't it?' she said. 'It keeps away the midges. The sun's on our backs, and the breeze is in our faces. Otherwise, we'd be roasting! Aren't we lucky to have it?'

The water was clear, clear. You could see right to the bottom.

'I've so many bad habits. I don't hold the rod right. I don't cast properly.' Snap. The line went out, straight as an arrow into the wind. 'Dan said to go on doing it the way I'm used to. A quick flick backwards, then forward pressure, bring the rod forward with force, lay the line down on the water in a long straight line . . . that's the correct method. I put pressure in the wrong places. Too much backward and not enough forward. Do the Wayana fish for their dinner, James?'

'With a bow and arrow.'

'Ah, yes. . . . Of course.'

'Patience is the key to success in fishing, I was told.'

'That's absolutely right.'

'A fisherman can learn from the heron.'

'Is your father still alive, James? I mean your real father.'

'Who knows? He went back to Germany a long time ago. I don't even know his name.'

'What about your mother – your real mother?'

'She may be. I haven't seen her since I left the jungle.'

'Do you have anything of hers?'

'A cross – a crucifix.'

'Do you wear it?'

'No.'

'Did she?'

'No. I don't know. She used to keep it in a little box.'

'Was she a Christian?'

'Maybe. Once. For one night.'

'Will you look for her when you go home?'

'Perhaps. I've thought about it, but I don't know whether I'll do it or not.'

'She'd be happy to know you survived.'

'Yes, but I'd be sad to learn she hasn't.'

'I don't know what's wrong,' she said, reeling in the line. 'Charlie said these lakes are full of fish.'

'I heard that the Shining Path gangs have dynamited the Andean lakes for food. Maybe all the fish have been blown to smithereens.'

'All those beautiful fish destroyed by a bomb – how disgusting.'

'When you're starving, your stomach doesn't let you think of the beauty of what you kill to eat.'

'I suppose I've never experienced real hunger myself.' Rosalinda began to take apart her fly rod. 'I don't know about this place. I agree with you, it is kind of spooky.'

I hadn't said anything, but the vast expressionless lake and the barrenness of the shore, where nothing grew, filled me with an unnamed dread. There were birds out there on the silvery water. We could see them swimming about and hear their plaintive cries, but nothing else moved. The threat of danger from the bandits, who could not be far away, suddenly became palpable. I could feel it rising within me, like a great invisible fish floating upwards towards an unsuspecting prey.

On the shore a man appeared.

Rosalinda grabbed my hand. 'Who's that?'

He had materialized from nowhere and was standing on a low round hill, looking at us.

My heart started pounding again. 'He's wearing a uniform. It must be one of the soldiers.'

97

Sunlight glinted off his binoculars.

'Why is he interested in us?' she said.

'The soldiers are interested in everybody these days, especially in Puno Province. Everyone here's a suspected terrorist.'

'Well, I don't like to be spied on. I feel like a bug under a microscope. Let's get out of here. We can visit the ruins.'

We left the lake on a path that led around the side of a long, low mountain. It was covered with sharp, flat, geometrically shaped rocks of a reddish-grey colour. Filmy sloughed-off snakeskins were draped over the rocks, so we walked carefully.

I picked up a stick. 'This place must be full of vipers,' I said.

The words were no sooner out of my mouth than a buzzing sound startled us. I thought it was an alarm clock going off.

'Rosalinda, watch out!'

A fat grey and brown rattlesnake was curled up against a rock. Its forked tongue flicked in and out as it looked at us with its sinister eyes, like two bits of polished coal. Its tail was going a mile a minute.

I dragged her back. 'Don't go near it!'

'It's a warning, isn't it? It doesn't want to kill us. It's telling us to stay away.'

'Yes, but if you'd stepped on it, it would have turned its head and sunk its fangs into your leg.'

We looked at the snake with mingled fear and fascination. It made no move against us. Rosalinda was right: the angry sound it was making may have saved our lives. We could have easily made a detour around it, but my animal instincts got the better of me, and I did the totally unnecessary thing. I picked up a rock.

'Are you going to kill it?'

'Yes.'

We both seized rocks and began to throw. The vibrations increased to an intolerable level. The rocks, thrown in a frenzy, mostly missed. When some began to hit, the snake abandoned its defensive position and attempted to slither away. The hail of sharp rocks soon cut him up, and he writhed in red as blood covered the rock. The deafening noise ceased, but we did not stop throwing until all but his tail was buried under a pile of stones.

'Do you want the rattle for a souvenir?' I said.

'Don't touch him! He might not be dead yet.'

Keeping our eyes peeled for more snakes, we hurried on our way. The path led to an opening in the side of the mountain which gaped at us like an enormous mouth. A stalactite hanging in the recesses resembled a grotesque tonsil.

'Shall we have a peek inside?'

'I'd rather not. . . .' Rosalinda took a step backwards. 'Caves make me feel claustrophobic. Besides, there may be more snakes inside, or bats. You don't know what's in there. Wouldn't it be a perfect place for terrorists to hide?'

'Not this near the hotel.'

'You say that, but you can't be sure.'

'Wait here. I'm going to have a look.'

'No, I won't. I'm coming with you.'

We climbed up to the cave's mouth, which must have been twenty or thirty feet high, and advanced cautiously inside. It was dark in there, and damp. The dripping walls reverberated with the growlings and grindings of some invisible creatures. We looked up and, as our eyes grew accustomed to the gloom, we made the discovery of the owls. There they were in their thousands, wing to wing along the walls and roof of the cave. They occupied every nook and cranny, clinging to the rocky façade, waiting out the day in the darkened cave. Row upon row of them, in close order, like an army in repose, they were growing restless for darkness to come. They reminded me of the men of the Shining Path, packed shoulder to shoulder in the booths of that *chicha* bar. Like the owls, they were awaiting the moment to emerge for the hunt and the kill.

'Watch out! Look where you're stepping!'

We looked down at our feet. The ground swarmed with thousands of shiny black beetles, dung-devourers that fed on the owl droppings, and with another cockroach-like insect, with the segmented body of a trilobite, that burrowed into the earth (powdered owl dung) at the first sign of danger (our feet).

'Let's get out of here!'

'These bugs can't hurt us. What's the rush?'

'There's someone in here!'

'Where?'

Rosalinda pointed. In the shadowy recesses of the cave I could make out the broad brown face of an Indian. He was standing or sitting behind a pile of rocks that had fallen from the ceiling, so that only his head and shoulders were visible. His face was framed by stone. His expression was not welcoming, nor was it threatening. It was that inimitable deadpan Indian gaze in which there is neither judgement nor curiosity nor fear. He wore a woollen cap with earflaps. His seemed to be the solemn, immutable face of Peru.

'That's Peru for you,' I said. 'You think you're out in the middle of nowhere, miles from anyone, when you realize that some silent brown face that seems to have sprung from the earth is watching you.'

'What do you think he's doing here?' asked Rosalinda.

'Maybe he lives here. Maybe this cave is his home.'

'Either that or he's a terrorist. Shall we speak to him?'

We didn't; we turned and beat a hurried retreat back to the light.

The path curled around the edge of an escarpment, where we were presented with a panoramic view of the valley below. The valley floor was dotted with dozens of little lakes (*lagunillas*) and was surrounded by low brown mountains like the one we were standing on. Lowering grey clouds capped the dusty mountains, truncating them, and did not let the sun in. Our eyes had a choice of grey or brown. Dull grey and dull brown: colours which did not excite the spirit. These were the colours of resignation, of the military, of drought, of dishwater, of mouldering excrement. The hills had been eroded by water, and veins of darker earth showed through in patterns resembling fish skeletons or upside-down root systems.

100

'These mountains remind me of the hills around Arequipa, where the shantytowns are,' Rosalinda said. 'James, why did the Indians leave this place?'

'Can't you see? This land couldn't support them.'

'We live in a country where poverty has gone completely out of control. Daddy's first priority is to revitalize the Andean economy, the way only *they* know how.'

'But can he?'

'He's a farmer. He's made a lifetime study of Indian agricultural methods. If he can't, nobody can. Look down there. This must be Altar Sacrificio. We're here.'

We followed the path downwards and came out on a flat paved area. Massive slabs of stone had been laid down so tightly against each other that we could hardly make out the crack or join. It was as though they had been welded or melted together. The area must have been about forty or fifty feet across and was enclosed on three unequal sides by a stone wall of ingeniously bizarre construction. The rocks, which were of all different shapes, had not been placed in uniformly horizontal and overlapping layers, like bricks, but had been joined together like the pieces of a gigantic jigsaw puzzle. No Roman logic dictated this construction; it was a child's idea of order, of putting impossible shapes together and making them fit; and it had been accomplished by supreme craftsmanship, patience, and plain hard work. Every few feet the wall was indented by trapezoidal-shaped niches where idols had once stood. The fourth side was open to the west, with the view of the valley, the encircling hills, and the brooding volcanoes in the distance.

We were struck by the appearance of a tall white rock, round on one side and almost flat on the other, that stood, nearly perpendicular but not quite, in pristine solitude close to the centre of the paved area.

Our footsteps echoed as we approached.

'This must be the altar where the human sacrifices were made.'

A brass plaque was imbedded in stone at the foot of the white rock.

The priests first read prayers with the victims. Then round about this mystic white stone (*sillar*) they laid great quantities of wood and set fire to it. When the fire blazed the victims' horrid howlings so unnerved the others waiting to be executed that some dropped dead. When the last rays of the setting sun strike the face of the rock, one can make out, with an ordinary magnifying glass, curious hieroglyphics inscribed on the volcanic surface, where the surviving victims were summarily beheaded, an obsidian axe being the preferred instrument of execution.

It is said that similar rituals are being revived today in remote Andean regions. *¿Quien sabe, senores?*

– Courtesy of 'Friends of the Andes', the Puno Province Archaeological and Historical Society.

We sat down by the stone and gazed across the valley. The asymmetrical proportions of the plaza, the fact that it was perfectly made but completely cockeyed, had a strangely soothing effect upon us. The place might once have echoed with screams, but I found it restful to be there. Despite the blood that had flowed, the fires that had scorched human flesh, and the unspeakable tortures inflicted, the atmosphere of Altar Sacrificio was redolent of peace and conducive to contemplation.

'It's hard to imagine, isn't it?' Rosalinda remarked after a few minutes. 'This place is so beautiful, and yet terrible things happened here.'

'Well, I guess the Incas believed that blood had to be spilled for beauty to survive.'

'But how can one even *think* about beauty when people are being killed?'

'I don't think they looked at it that way. They viewed it as a necessary price that had to be paid.'

'Well, I'm not about to give anyone who deliberately tortures the benefit of the doubt. The Incas may have created a fantastic civilization, but this part of it was barbaric.'

All of a sudden the sun, which had been absent most of the afternoon, sank below the cloud layer and, caught in a crotch of hills, sent out a blistering light that coated the valley and turned all the *lagunillas* pink. There was a rainstorm in the distance, a crack of lightning and, in dramatic response, a country church bell began to clank somewhere. One could see for miles and miles. The Renaissance painters, taxing their imaginations to display the glory of the Lord, could not have improved on the scene before us. As the lightning flashed again the pitiful church bell histrionically answered.

'James, quick, let's see if we can see the inscriptions on the rock!'

I jumped down and looked. I had no magnifying glass, and the hieroglyphics, if they still existed, were obliterated by the large, bold words:

EL PUEBLO MUERE DE HAMBRE

'I don't see anything.'

'Look up there, James. On the hill!'

The cactus trees, standing tall and solitary, seemed to prefer the high rocky ground. Silhouetted against the evening sky, they dominated the ridge above us. Rosalinda was pointing at the soldiers crouching among them. There were two now, watching us through binoculars.

'I don't like this.' I took her hand. 'Let's go back.'

15

We were glad to see the Reina Victoria again. Amid so much desolation, the hotel seemed like the Rock of Gibraltar. After the episode with the snake, the face in the cave, the forlorn and forbidding appearance of the *laguna*, and especially the persistent surveillance by the soldiers, it was a relief to be back inside.

Our gloomy mood fell away when we entered the hotel and saw Dot. We didn't object when she made a fuss over us; we were happy to be her children.

'Come on upstairs and see our nest.' She winked at the grinning Indian behind the desk. 'When I told Melanio you were Charlie's granddaughter, he showed me the Presidential Suite.' She led the way to the stairs. 'Do you know, he's kept it just like it was when your grandfather used to come here to fish, as a kind of shrine. Melanio!' she shouted. 'Mix up the medicine!'

'You told him who Rosalinda was?' I asked, a little sharply.

'Why, uh, yes, I did.' Dot looked puzzled.

'This is guerrilla country, Dot. If the Shining Path learned the President's daughter was in the hotel, they'd be swarming around here like a pack of hyenas.'

'I'm sorry. . . . That was stupid of me.'

'I'm sure the hotel staff are loyal to Charlie.' To make Dot feel better, Rosalinda made light of my concern. 'Besides, the soldiers are here to protect us. Come on.'

She was eager to see where Charlie used to stay. She tiptoed in and looked expectantly around. The Presidential Suite consisted of a large sitting room, half of which was occupied by a pool table, and two adjoining bedrooms. The wooden furniture was hand-made and heavy; it had that rustic look you might expect to see in a fishing lodge. There was a bar in one corner and a card table with a light hanging over it in another. Poker chips were stacked on a shelf. A pair of ancient pinball machines stood side by side, like an elderly couple. Stuffed fish decorated the walls, along with some corny framed sayings.

> HOMBRE CASADO
> BURRO DOMADO*

> SOY SOLTERO
> LA CASADA ES MI MUJER†

> EL MATRIMONIO ES
> LA UNICA GUERRA
> DONDE LOS EMENIGOS
> DUERMEN JUNTOS‡

A log fire blazed cheerfully in the fireplace, but the lights hanging over the pool and poker tables gave off a hard, garish glare. A moosehead with a cigar stuck in its mouth struck a note of jocular vulgarity. There were large sand ashtrays for cigars, with the presidential seal still imprinted on the surface of the sand. A spittoon occupied every corner. The atmosphere of Charlie's old quarters was spartan and masculine; it looked like a dingy saloon.

Rosalinda walked around and inspected everything, as though she were in a museum. A frown creased her brow. I could see that her image of Charlie's fishing trips did not tally

*Married man = tame donkey
†I'm single – the married one is my wife
‡Marriage is the only war where the enemies sleep together

with this scene of bachelor revels with his cronies.

She let out a little shriek when she opened the door of a closet that was full of women's clothes.

'Did he have girls in here?'

'Girls, boys . . . everybody dress up for parties.' Melanio was standing in the doorway, holding a tray full of *pisco* sours. 'Sometimes even Meester Charlie . . .'

Rosalinda turned away. She didn't want to hear any more. Melanio put down the tray, pulled out a photo of himself and Charlie, and proudly showed it to her. She glanced at it, sank into a chair, gazed despondently at the fire, and refused a drink.

Dot sat down beside her. 'Look at it this way, dearie. He came up here to relax and get away from the affairs of state, didn't he? He had a lot of heavy responsibilities, and he couldn't fish all the time, could he? You can't fish at night. Can you blame him for wanting to have a little fun?'

'I know, but it all seems so sordid. Our fishing trips were never like this.' Rosalinda seemed close to tears. 'It was just us and nature. Sometimes we didn't even have to talk.'

'I know, I know. Look, when a man is with his granddaughter, he's going to be on his best behaviour. For him she's an ideal of youth and beauty. She represents the future at its brightest. She even makes him feel younger and less afraid of death, because after he's dead, part of him is going forward into the future with her. She's going to bring out the best in him because she gives him hope and because he's proud of her. A man like Charlie . . . a powerful man, President of his country . . . he's going to have many sides, some good and some . . . not so good. A politician does many things in his life, a lot of them good things, but maybe some he's not so proud of and would rather forget. And when he's with his chums on a fishing trip, he's probably at his worst. He needs to let off steam. He uses foul language, he says things he wouldn't say at home, he probably drinks too much. He does things he wouldn't want his family to know about, but it's all harmless. It's just grown men acting like they were boys again. It may seem silly and asinine, but it doesn't hurt anybody.'

Rosalinda nodded, but she didn't look convinced that Charlie's fishing trips were entirely innocent. They didn't seem that way to me, either. If he could be crude when he was enjoying himself, what sort of baseness was he capable of when he was conducting the affairs of state? That was the question Rosalinda seemed to be asking herself, too. I was glad not to have to be the one to tell her about the burying alive of the miners at Cerro de Pasco, the massacre at Huanta, or any other atrocities he might have been responsible for.

When the sun went down, the temperature plummeted and a cold wind began to moan round the corners of the hotel. There was no escaping the dust. It blew in under the doors and through the broken windows as the old hotel creaked and rocked in the rising gale.

When we came downstairs, we found a warning from the Ministry of Agriculture we hadn't noticed before.

La Cueva de las Lechuzas

The cave is saturated with mushrooms, causing a condition technically known as histo-plasmosis, a hole-in-the-lung-making disease whose action on the human organism produces *trastornos de gravedad* (serious disturbances). The university has isolated it and is now looking for an antidote, so until it finds one

STAY OUT

'You see, James? I knew we shouldn't have gone in that cave. They should have put this sign at the entrance to the cave, not here.'

'If they had, the Indian in the cave would have ripped it out and used it as firewood. That's Peru for you.'

'Do you think the poor man knows about this disease?'

'I doubt it.'

'Someone should tell him.'

'I agree, but I don't think even the threat of a death sentence would move him. The cave is probably his home, and he's got nowhere else to live.'

16

Dot treated us to dinner. She tried her best to make it a jolly meal. She cracked jokes with the waiters who gathered around the table, but she couldn't get Rosalinda to cheer up.

'Oh, come on,' she said, using a mock-gruff tone of voice to mask her affection. 'Remember – we're going to the circus tonight. And who remembered to make a New Year's resolution?'

Before anyone could answer, the door banged open, and two soldiers came into the hotel. They called Melanio over and started talking to him. They were asking him questions but they were looking at us. They carried guns – kalashnikovs and pistols strapped to their waists.

Their uniforms were scruffy 'and torn and hadn't been washed in a long time. Instead of army boots they wore sandals made out of old rubber tyres. On their heads were woollen caps with earflaps, and shapeless felt hats.

'They don't look like proper soldiers to me,' I whispered to Rosalinda. 'I hope to God Melanio has the good sense not to tell them who you are. They look like soldiers who have gone native, or natives who have disguised themselves as soldiers.'

'What did they want?' I asked Melanio after they had gone. 'Were they asking questions about us?'

'They wanted to know the identity of Señorita Calderón.'

'What did you tell them?'

'I tell them . . . she . . . English señorita travelling with friends.'

'That's the stuff, Melanio. You see?' Dot smiled. 'He didn't let the cat out of the bag.'

The menu came in a leather-bound book with translations in four languages.

'What are horse eggs?' Dot wanted to know.

Melanio announced that the day's speciality was grilled bull.

'That's it then,' Dot shut her book. 'Make mine rare.'

'I'll have pan-fried rainbow trout,' Rosalinda said.

'The Shining Path came with dynamite and blew all the fish out of the *laguna*,' Melanio explained. 'None left now.'

'What did I tell you?'

'Did they have to kill all the fish?'

'When the *bomba* goes off, señorita, every fish dies.'

The meat came in big, thick, irregularly cut pieces, burned black on the outside and bloody red and still bleeding on the inside. Dot tried cutting hers with a Swiss army knife, but even little pieces were too tough to chew. When she complained, Melanio perfunctorily picked up her plate, opened the window, and hurled the meat into the dark. There was a hideous snarling of dogs.

'Now, was that necessary?'

Rosalinda, who had been sawing away, put down her knife and fork. 'I can't eat mine, either.' Fortunately, Melanio knew how to make an omelette. Then, when we had finished eating, he came in carrying a little cake with a candle burning in the centre.

'Surprise, surprise!' Dot led the singing of the birthday song. 'Now make a wish. Don't tell anybody or it won't come true.'

'That man in the cave,' Rosalinda blew out the candle. 'I can't stop thinking about him. His life may be in danger.'

'There's no point in worrying about him,' I said. 'He's either got this histo-plasmosis, or he hasn't. If he hasn't got it by now, he'll probably never get it. And if he's got it, there's no cure for it, so we can't do anything about it, can we?'

'Someone should warn him. I told you we shouldn't have gone in there.'

'I'll tell you what,' Dot said. 'Tomorrow morning, before the train leaves, I'll walk with you to the cave and you can tell the man about the disease.'

'All right.' Dot's suggestion put Rosalinda's mind at ease. 'Thank you, Dot.'

'When Thad died, some of my friends wrote me off,' Dot said. 'They pronounced me dead, said it was all over for me. But being here with you two has given me a new lease on life. Let's go to the circus.'

The wind tried to tear the clothes off our backs as we made our way across the eroded plain. Now I understood why the tent was located in a pit – to escape the cold blast of air that blew down from the Andes each night to scour the land and suck out its moisture. Only the cactus trees survived, and they rubbed each other bald in groaning protest.

Attracted by a line of flickering fires, we made a detour by the train tracks where the engineer was working with an acetylene torch to repair the broken rail. A row of Indian children, solemn as acolytes, held lanterns so the men could see.

'*Buenas noches, señores,*' a voice called cheerfully from the caboose.

'Keep an eye on those tyres,' Dot admonished.

'*Si, señora!*' Eustaquio leaned through the window and saluted. '*Con mucho gusto, con cariño, con. . . .*' He fell backwards. There was a crash.

'He's drunk.'

We passed by the Indian encampment. The fires roared in the wind. Rotund women in derby hats were roasting hunks of bull heart on wire skewers. There were children everywhere, babies crying and babies sleeping.

'Look at those mountain girls with their huge black eyes. And their children – they're like dolls,' Rosalinda remarked.

'There's something so sweet and vulnerable and hopeless about these people,' Dot said. 'It almost breaks your heart.'

'It's true,' Rosalinda agreed. 'They have everything, and they have nothing.'

'Once they had everything,' I said. 'Now they have nothing.'

'When do you mean, James?' Rosalinda asked. 'Before the Spanish came to Peru?'

'Yes.'

'Then I suppose you agree with the Shining Path that Peru belongs to the Indians?'

'On this particular point I agree with them, and so does your father.'

'But not with their violence.'

'Never.'

Hurrying back and forth to the well, the diminutive hatted women, with long skirts and great bundles, led or carried children with bright red, chapped cheeks.

'Their eyes seem to see things we don't see,' Rosalinda said. 'They know things we don't know.'

'Indian eyes have that worried look from centuries of trotting along sierra trails,' I said. 'From looking upwards at the looming cliffs and the snowfields ready to plunge down on them.'

'Those are eyes that expect the worst to happen,' Dot said.

'Yes, and here in the Andes it usually does.'

Andean seagulls fluttered about like lost souls in the darkness. Llamas grazed in the firelight. Drinking *chicha* from a jug, a group of Indian men were sitting on discarded millstones left over from the time of the Spanish. I had a headache, and my heart was beating fast. Was it nerves, or a case of *siroche*? Wrapping ourselves against the cold, biting wind from the Altiplano, we hurried on to the circus.

The Indians from the train had paid a penny each to get inside the tent. They sat in a big circle with their backs to the canvas. Some were perched on the edge of the tent to keep the icy air from blowing in. The entire tent fabric rocked and swayed in the gale, and from time to time jerked convulsively, like something alive. In the centre of the circle a lantern on a stool illuminated the Indians. Their faces were flushed from drinking *chicha* and eating meat. Powdery dust filtered through the air. No one spoke. All was quiet but for the steady munching and spitting by the Indians. The women were chewing pumpkin seeds; the men's cheeks bulged with coca leaves. A hissing, sighing marine sound rose and fell with the volume of wind.

The keeper led his animal in. The Indians gasped in amazement. None of them had seen an elephant before. A

111

woman screamed and had to be held down, but most were mesmerized by the sight of the gigantic beast.

Nuria knew a few tricks. She stood on two legs and balanced on buckets. Her bulk filled the centre of the tent, and when she walked in a circle her back brushed against the roof, bringing down more dust. A long shadow and a wave of fear followed her wherever she went, the Indians cringing and flattening themselves against the tent wall.

'Do you know why I'm wearing these green clothes, ladies and gentlemen?' the keeper asked in a loud voice. 'Green is the colour of Allah. . . .'

'It's also the colour of hope,' Rosalinda whispered.

'. . . and Allah is the big god in Africa where this animal comes from. . . .'

'Doesn't he know it's an Indian elephant?'

'Allah is a big god in India, too, isn't he?' I said.

'Of all the creatures in the world, this animal is the largest and lives the longest,' the keeper continued sonorously. 'She has the best memory. There is nothing that she does not know. There is a magic word that will cause this animal to remember the world before man was born.'

The keeper turned to face where we were sitting. He was staring at Rosalinda. 'Besides myself, there is only one other person in this tent who knows the magic word that will make the elephant tell its secret.'

The eyes of every Indian gazed expectantly at Rosalinda. There was a prolonged silence broken only by the sound of the wind, and the canvas flapping.

'Salt!' Rosalinda shouted.

Nuria reared back on her hind legs. Her head made a bulge in the top of the tent. Her ears were flapping and she trumpeted like a locomotive.

There was pandemonium. Within seconds the tent was empty. The Indians had bolted into the night.

Besides ourselves, the only ones left were a group of soldiers who did not run. They sat in a row across the ring from us. They wore ponchos over their uniforms. They had been there the whole time, but we hadn't seen them. They only materialized when the crowd fled. They were all full-blooded Indians, and they were looking at us. Sitting just behind and peering over their shoulders was the grinning rat-face of The Armadillo.

The elephant seemed to shrink in size as we stared at each other.

'Well, do you think they got their money's worth?' the keeper called as he led his animal away.

Rosalinda had got to her feet and was walking across the ring. She was standing in front of the soldiers. 'Eduardito, is that you?' she asked.

A very swarthy Indian got up and stood formally before her. Long black hair fell to his shoulders. His face was handsome in a primitive, Mongolian way, with black eyes recessed behind high, swollen cheekbones.

'Yes. I am Eduardito,' we heard him say.

'Do you know who I am?' She doffed her hat.

'You are Rosalinda.'

17

We all trooped back to the hotel. Rosalinda and Eduardito walked on ahead. He had a bad limp. We could hear her asking about it. Dot and I came next, with The Armadillo and the two 'soldiers' bringing up the rear.

'I don't like it,' I whispered. 'He may be Rosalinda's old team-mate, but he's committed all kinds of crimes, including rape. He's on every wanted list in the country.'

'What's he doing here?' Dot asked.

'That's what I'd like to know, too. The Shining Path never comes out into the open like this.'

'Are they the ones who blew up the tracks?'

'It must be them.'

'Why did they do it?' she asked. 'It doesn't make any sense. Rosalinda said the train is scheduled to stop here anyhow.'

'My guess is that they stopped the train because they didn't want anyone to know what was going on here. They did it to make sure I got off. See that scrawny fellow behind us? The one in the raincoat? They call him The Armadillo. He used to be one of Dr Morales's storm troopers at the university – you know, the head of the Shining Path. Yesterday he found out I was Uncle Joshua's nephew, and he's been following me ever since. Dr Morales must have got in touch with Eduardito somehow, and Eduardito stopped the train to grab me. But now that he's discovered Rosalinda is here, I don't think he's interested in me any more. He must be stunned by the enormity of the prize that's fallen into his hands.'

'He better not touch a hair on that girl's head.'

'They've got guns, Dot. He can do what he wants.'

'We've got to get her away from here.'

'Yes, but how? The train is the only link with the outside world.'

For a while Rosalinda and Eduardito played the soccer game in the hotel lobby. Dot and I sat on the sofa, as dust swirled in under the door and coasted across the floor.

'This is too weird,' I said. 'Watching Rosalinda play that game with Eduardito gives me the creeps. While he twiddles those knobs and scoots the ball around, he's only got two thoughts in his head – whether he's going to kill her or kidnap her – and us, too.'

Eduardito's friends stayed on the other sofa. They had taken apart their kalashnikovs and were cleaning them. They fondled these weapons not in a threatening but in a loving sort of way, yet they also meant to show us who was boss. They were mere teenagers, these beardless Indian gunmen, but already they wore the ancient fixed expressions that have been depicted in Andean artwork from time immemorial. Their unchanging faces once worshipped the Inca; maybe they still did. Now they'd become bandits and revolutionaries in a belated effort, centuries overdue, to expel the unwanted invader from their land.

Dot looked confused. It hadn't sunk in yet that these teenagers were terrorists. 'Everything seems normal so far, doesn't it?' she whispered hopefully. 'I mean, except their guns.'

'Nothing's normal. Don't be lulled into a false sense of security.' I thought to myself about the incident the previous week when some Shining Path guerrillas had stopped a bus on the road between Ayacucho and Andahuaylas. They had singled out two French tourists from the other passengers and had shot them by the side of the road. Just like that. For no reason at all.

When I glanced at The Armadillo, he nodded towards the row of grinning skulls and gave me a little smile. His satisfaction unnerved me, because I knew what cruel punishment he and the others thought Rosalinda and her family deserved.

'What are they waiting for?' Dot asked.

'They can take their time, because we're completely cut off here. Nobody in the outside world thinks anything is wrong. There are no roads, just a few Andean tracks winding among the volcanoes that only the Indians know about, and no telephone. Isn't that why Charlie liked Lagunas Lagunillas, because nobody could get at him here? Since the train is supposed to make a scheduled stop here, as far as the outside world is concerned, everything is normal. The train is always late, so the authorities in Juliaca won't be concerned – not yet. Uncle Joshua thinks Rosalinda is on the train, and he isn't worried. Dr Morales must know Eduardito is here, but he may not know Rosalinda is. So Eduardito can take his time about making up his mind what he's going to do with us, because no one can escape.'

'I have an idea how we can.'

'How?'

'In that army truck we saw by the railroad tracks.'

Rosalinda and Eduardito had stopped playing the soccer game and were holding a little conference. She walked over to us, while he went to speak with the other terrorists.

'We're going to have a real game of soccer,' she announced. 'Outside.'

'We've got to get you out of here!' Dot whispered. She seemed to have grasped the seriousness of the situation.

'What's wrong with you, Rosalinda?' I said. 'Don't you realize that he could demand a ransom for you that would make Atahualpa's room full of gold seem like pocket change?'

'I've already talked it over with him.' Rosalinda replied, apparently calm, but her voice was tense. 'It was the first thing I asked him – whether he intended to kidnap me. He said no. He has nothing against me, he said. He's an old friend.'

'He doesn't have to kidnap you,' I said, 'because we already are his prisoners, whether we like it or not. There's no way we can get out of here. They have guns and we don't, so they can do what they want with us.'

'Until tonight at nine-thirty,' Dot added, 'which is when the train is supposed to pull into Juliaca. Johnny will be there to meet me. If it doesn't arrive, there will be an alert and the soldiers will come.'

'Listen,' Rosalinda whispered. 'Listen to me. He still loves soccer. He hasn't played it in ages. It's the great love of his life. It'll put him in a good mood to play. So come and join in. It'll seem more friendly if we all play together.'

'Why should we care what mood these bandits are in,' Dot asked under her breath, 'when they can kill us any time they want?'

'He's not going to kill anyone.'

'How can you be so sure?'

Rosalinda's reply left us stunned. 'Because he loves me.'

'What? How do you know that?'

'He has always loved me. And I . . . when I was younger, when we played on the team together . . . I loved him.'

'What? Are you crazy?' I said. 'An Indian? How can you love an Indian? It's impractical, it's almost illegal, your family wouldn't tolerate it, and besides, it doesn't make sense. Look. Look at me. I'm the result when a white person loves an Indian. Is this what you want? Someone who looks like me?'

Rosalinda's lips trembled. 'That's why I was sent away to England, because I loved him. I had to have an abortion in London. And I was kicked out of school – because I ran off hoping to see him play. Now you know the truth. Come on.'

Dot and I looked at each other, speechless.

'What the heck is going on?'

I shrugged. 'I don't know.'

We stepped outside into the windy darkness. The night was as black as ink. Far away a volcano was shooting sparks into the sky as a blob of orange lava oozed downwards. Down by the tracks campfires flickered.

'I've never played soccer in my life. I can't run a step,' Dot grumbled. 'No one can see a thing.'

Eduardito had already given orders to one of his men, who now came back in the truck. The lights lit up the front of the hotel, including the flat area where the staff played soccer. The twin piles of whitewashed stones looked like tombs.

A ball was found. Next came the problem of choosing sides. Rosalinda insisted on playing in the same team with Eduardito, like in the old days. I suppose she was right. She did seem to exert a certain hold over him. He never took his eyes off her. I was named captain of the other team and chose Dot, along with The Armadillo and another of the terrorists.

The game proceeded sporadically. Even with the light from the truck (only one worked) shining across the ground, it wasn't easy to see. The wind blew the ball around, and the dust erupted in explosions wherever we ran. The terrorists' holsters slapped against their thighs as they chased the ball.

I had a chance to score but kicked the ball wide of the goal.

'Play like you mean it!' Rosalinda shouted as she ran by. 'Our lives may depend on it!'

When the ball went out of bounds, it invariably rolled into a hole or gully. The game was halted while Eduardito sent one of the terrorists to retrieve it. He didn't want any of us running away.

Eduardito hobbled badly. Rosalinda passed the ball to him every chance she got. He couldn't run fast, but when he had possession of the ball, it was hard to get it away from him. They were both out of practice, but they were still much better than anyone else.

Once I bumped into Eduardito and knocked him off balance. At that moment I could have snatched the pistol from his holster, but I didn't have the nerve. I played it safe because I was scared of getting hurt or dying. Eduardito spotted me glancing at the gun and read my intentions. Seeing I was afraid gave him confidence.

When he scored the first goal, Rosalinda hugged him.

'Look at her. . . . ' Dot was completely out of breath. She was leaning against one of the piles of stones and could hardly stand up. 'Embracing the man who might kill her. . . . Do you think she really loves him?'

'Don't you see she's trying to flatter him every chance she gets? Here – give me the ball. I bet she's as scared as we are, but maybe she's right – maybe this is the way to save our skins.'

'It'll never work.'

'What will?'

'I don't know – nothing,' Dot suddenly made a choking noise. 'Oh dear, it's nine-fifteen. Johnny will be at the station in Juliaca,' she sobbed. 'I'm afraid I'll never see him again!'

'Hold on – don't give up yet. I don't think Eduardito's made up his mind what to do with us.'

'The soldiers will be here in the morning looking for the train. Maybe Johnny will be with them.'

'If Eduardito's still around when the soldiers arrive, his goose'll be cooked,' I said encouragingly.

'That truck is our only chance.'

'You could be right, Dot.'

After a while the Indians began to reappear. Attracted by the sight of people running around in the light, they had wandered over from their camp by the railroad tracks. A line of spectators enclosed the soccer ground. The sight of them inspired Rosalinda, and she invited them to join the game. Soon there were two complete teams chasing the ball.

I was happy to relinquish my place. While I caught my breath, Dot beckoned. She was standing by the truck. It was painted in camouflage colours and had a military licence plate.

'What do you think of the game now?' I said. 'The rumour's going round the Indians that the daughter of the President-elect of the Republic is playing on the same team as the most wanted bandit in Puno Province.'

'Look at this.' Dot was peering through the truck window. 'There's a radio in here.'

'That must be how Eduardito dodges the soldiers, by tuning into their frequencies and learning where they are.'

'Not this radio. I've just had a look at it. It's supposed to be hooked up to the truck battery, but I can see it isn't. The lead is loose. My hunch is that Eduardito has never used this thing because he doesn't know how it works.'

'Do you know how it works, Dot?'

'Thad was a ham radio operator in Cerro de Pasco. That's how we kept in touch with our friends back home. He taught me how to use it.'

'Dot, if you can make this radio go, we can tell the outside world what's happening here!'

'It's a US army radio. It ought to work, unless it's been damaged in some way I can't see in the dark. Look at this.' She led me round to the back of the truck and lifted up a tarpaulin.

It was dark inside. 'What is it?'

She shone a pencil flashlight on something metal lying on the bottom of the truck. 'That's a machine gun, or part of one.'

'Eduardito must have stolen it from the army,' I said.

'The tripod is missing. It needs to sit on something that will soak up the recoil before it can be fired.'

I was impressed at Dot's unexpected resourcefulness. 'How do you know these things, Dot?'

'Johnny was a Green Beret in Vietnam. He used to fire one of these guns from a helicopter. He showed me pictures. He said it kicks like a mule. I wish he were here now. You can bet your life he'd know what to do.'

'For God's sake, Dot, turn that light off! Don't let them know we're snooping around.'

'Maybe we should let the air out of the tyres so they can't get away.'

'I'll tell you why you better not. We mustn't do anything that'll prevent them from leaving this place. Rosalinda is trying to make friends with Eduardito, and if it works, maybe he'll go away and leave us alone.'

'I don't want them to escape. I hope they get caught. Bandits are making the roads dangerous for Johnny, too.'

'Look, Dot, please don't do anything to antagonize them while Rosalinda is here. If anything happened to her, it wouldn't just be a tragedy for her family. Imagine the national calamity if she were kidnapped with Uncle Joshua about to take office. The army would step in, and there'd be cruel repressions, which is just what the Shining Path want. It'd be the end of democracy in Peru, probably for ever. Let's wait until she's safe. Look at them now. They're playing soccer together. It's a game they love. Soccer is probably the only game in the world that capitalists and terrorists both like to play. It's the only thing they can agree on. A lot of water has passed under the bridge, but they're still friends, thanks to soccer. The more he gets to like her, the less he'll be inclined to hurt her. I bet he's thought of it. It's bound to be going through his mind – he could twist her arm behind her back, and all Peru would be on its knees. We're at his mercy, and our only chance is Rosalinda. Maybe she can charm him or talk him out of what Dr Morales wants.' A thought struck me. 'I'm glad the radio doesn't work, because if he could get in touch with Dr Morales we'd have had it. Morales is ruthless. He would order Eduardito to kill us and hold her hostage until his demands are met, and then probably kill her, too, anyway. So put out that light and leave this truck alone. She's fighting for her life – for all our lives. Let them play.'

18

After the game broke up, Rosalinda came over to us. Her cheeks were pink from running, her hair was flying, and her eyes were shining with a kind of wild inspiration. We were all out of our minds with fear and uncertainty.

'Eduardito and I are going for a walk,' she announced breathlessly.

'What for?' I asked. 'Where to?'

'I don't know. It's his idea.'

'I don't like it – the two of you alone together,' Dot said. 'James said he's wanted for rape.'

'He wants to talk.'

'He's shrewd, that boy,' Dot said. 'I can see it in his eyes. He's scheming all the time, even when he's playing soccer.'

'Dot's right,' I said.

But Rosalinda was adamant. 'No, I've got to listen to what he has to say. I'm going now. And by the way – Eduardito says his friends are hungry. Can Melanio get them something to eat?'

'Take this.' Dot handed her the Swiss army knife. 'If he tries anything funny, stick it under his ribs and twist. The kidney is the best spot, here, near the small of the back where it's soft. Just jab it in and pull. Take it! It's as sharp as a razor.'

Dot and I went back to the hotel. The staff had vanished. We sat down on the sofa again. The Armadillo and the others followed us in and flopped down on the sofa opposite. It was a routine we were following, as though we were rehearsing for the theatre. This time they started arguing among themselves. I listened for a while.

'What are they saying?' Dot whispered.

'They don't like Rosalinda and Eduardito going off, either.' I translated surreptitiously while the fight went on. 'The one who followed me – The Armadillo – thinks we should be tied up . . . we all should be tied up and . . .'

'Tied up and what, James?' She was staring at her hands as though she had never seen them before. She looked terrified. Tears trickled down her cheeks. 'I don't want to be shot. I like my life. I don't care if nobody else does. I have Johnny to think about. I'm all he's got. I want to see Johnny again.' She reached for my hand. Hers was shaking. It was jerking back and forth.

'I don't think they know what they're going to do with us yet,' I lied. 'They haven't made up their minds,' I repeated like a parrot. 'They're waiting for Eduardito to decide. The Armadillo is angry the way Eduardito is handling things. It's too casual. He thinks Eduardito wants to have his cake and eat it, too.'

'You mean. . . ?'

'I think he means that Eduardito wants to make love to Rosalinda before he makes up his mind.'

'Rape and then kill her? Oh God, I can't believe this is happening. Why did we let her go off with him?'

'We had no choice, Dot.'

'Our fate is being decided by those two children,' she moaned. 'If he gets on top of her I hope she sticks the knife in and pulls. . . .' She grunted. '*Hard!*'

We sat there for a few more minutes. It seemed like hours. The terrorists got out their kalashnikovs again and started wiping them.

'Who's hungry?' Dot suddenly asked in a loud voice. 'I've got to do something,' she said to me. 'Who's for some sandwiches?' she shouted at the terrorists.

The terrorists looked at each other. The Armadillo motioned for one of them to accompany Dot into the kitchen. When Eduardito was away, he was in charge. . . .

This waiting was making me nervous, too. I walked over to the glass case that contained the skulls. Each skull had a hole about an inch square cut in the top of it, made by crosshatching incisions with the centre square removed. In three of the five skulls a thin shell of bone had grown back, re-covering the hole. In one the bone had partially grown back. In the fifth, the hole was wide open.

THE ANCIENT ART OF TREPANNING

The incisions in these craniums were made by Inca surgeons using obsidian scalpels to relieve migraine, remove tumours, or to take pressure off the brain where the skull had been broken by a war club. An anaesthetic was prepared from coca leaves, and a tourniquet was twisted tightly around the crown of the head to deaden pain and to reduce the supply of blood to the scalp. In exhibits 101–103 the incisions have closed up, indicating that the patients made complete recoveries. Exhibit 104 lived for several years, while 105 died shortly after the operation. Modern surgeons using the most advanced methods have not matched what the Inca doctors once achieved with stone scalpels and the distinctive 'tic-tac-toe' approach: *a technique that enabled the living skull to grow back*.
Exhibit courtesy of Friends of the Andes.

Dot came back into the room carrying a large wooden salad bowl piled high with popcorn. 'Here's your dinner, boys,' she said with exaggerated friendliness. 'Dig in.'

At the sound of her voice The Armadillo's eyes flashed. It was the furtive look of an animal caught unawares. But he grinned when he saw the popcorn.

'Fucky-fucky,' he said, mimicking the tones of a tough Callao whore, as he grabbed a handful of popcorn. He made a circle with the forefinger and thumb of one hand and shoved the forefinger of his other hand through it. 'Telephone! Vat 69!'

Dot passed the popcorn again. 'Come on, there's plenty for everybody!' Her enthusiasm puzzled me.

The Armadillo was pointing at the skulls again. 'Her and her and you. When we finish with you there will be eight skulls on that shelf. Not with square holes in them but with round ones.' He patted his gun.

Encouraged by Dot, the terrorists were wolfing down the popcorn.

'I've been thinking about that radio,' I whispered to Dot when she sat down beside me. 'If Rosalinda can distract him long enough, maybe you can use the radio to call for help. Are you sure you know how to use it?'

'I've never operated an army radio before, but I suppose I can try,' Dot said. Yet she seemed to have lost interest in the radio. It was the sickening spectacle of the terrorists gulping down popcorn that fascinated her. 'I put rat poison in,' she remarked casually.

'What?'

'Sitting on the pantry shelf next to the popcorn was a box full of pink powder with a skull and crossbones on it. So far no one's noticed the taste.'

My mind was racing out of control. Rat poison! In the jungle there lived a timid slow-moving rat called *marutopi*. We children used to catch them with our bare hands. As soon as we grabbed one, it stopped breathing and played dead. We had to give it a reassuring cuddle and a scratch behind the ears, to show it we didn't mean any harm, because the *marutopi*, when faced with a hopeless situation, sometimes held its breath for so long that it did in fact die. The *marutopi*'s strategy to elude pain, which we children used to laugh at, now made sense: how else were we going to dodge this trap?

Just then Rosalinda appeared in the doorway.

'You're back!' Dot jumped up. 'Are you all right?'

She walked over and handed Dot the knife.

'You've been gone for ages!' Dot said. 'Did he. . . ?'

'He didn't touch me. On our way to the Indian encampment by the railway tracks I told him about your son, Dot, distributing books for the poor people around Cuzco. Eduardito's a hero for them, you know. Everywhere we went, they ran up to him. "Eduardito! Eduardito!" Like he was Pelé or Maradona.'

'Listen, you crazy girl,' Dot growled. 'James has a plan, and we need your help.'

'What is it?'

'Do you think you can get Eduardito and his friends drunk while Dot uses his radio to call for help?'

'I don't think we'll need to do that because he's going to give himself up.'

Dot and I looked at each other in amazement. 'Did he tell you that?'

'On the way back here I said to him, Eduardito, if you want to help those people, you'll never succeed by being Robin Hood. Sooner or later, I said, the army is going to catch you, or someone will betray you. Sooner or later, they'll shoot you down or string you up. And what will you have accomplished? You'll be a legend in Puno Province, but the people will still be hungry. A new era is dawning in Peru, I told him. Next week my father is going to be sworn in as President. I know you like him. You told me yourself he was nice to you. He got you that scholarship at the university. My father thinks Peru belongs to the Indians, like you do. His plans for reform don't differ much from those of Dr Morales. He has secret dreams for Peru no one knows about because they're too radical. I know he'll tell you. Maybe you can even advise him. This trip has convinced *me* that I have to help him. I've seen the poverty. I know now how miserable people are. I can't go to Bolivia now; I'm going back to Arequipa. Daddy will come and get me. Come with me, Eduardito, I said to him. Daddy is going to free all the political prisoners as soon as he takes office. He hasn't said so publicly, but that's what he plans to do. If you give yourself up, he'll grant you amnesty, too. I'll tell him he has to. Then you can work side by side for a better Peru.'

Dot was sceptical. 'So what was Robin Hood's reaction to that high-minded speech?'

'He said he would think about it. He said he might give himself up, but only to Daddy, and only if Daddy comes here.'

'Comes *here*?' I repeated. 'You were away in England too long, Rosalinda. You've lost touch with reality. This is not a scene out of *Pride and Prejudice*. Eduardito is a terrorist responsible for a series of violent crimes, not a naughty boy who needs to be spanked.'

'How is he going to give himself up to your father?' Dot asked.

'Daddy can come here in his helicopter. We're going to call him on Eduardito's radio. I know he'll come and get me, and Eduardito will surrender when he gets here.'

'Do you mean to tell me,' I said, 'that Eduardito is stupid enough to get on the radio and tell the world where he is? The soldiers will be here in no time, and that will be the end of Eduardito.'

'No. He's not going to call. I am.'

'You? You are?'

'Yes, I'm going to get in touch with Daddy at Juanpablo.'

Eduardito, meanwhile, had come into the hotel. He flashed us a smile, briefly. The impact of that smile was like a ray of light in the darkness. It gave us hope. Suddenly, I felt that Rosalinda was right after all. Then that Indian mask of seriousness and sadness came down again, as he started conferring with the others.

'He may not want to give himself up when his friends start getting sick,' I said.

'He's going to eat the popcorn!' Dot whispered excitedly.

'Who is?' Rosalinda asked.

'Eduardito.'

'Dot put rat poison in it,' I said.

Whirling around, Rosalinda walked quickly across the room to the soccer table where the popcorn bowl was sitting, and knocked it to the floor.

'I'm sorry,' she said to Eduardito. 'I'm sure there's plenty more in the kitchen.'

Almost immediately a violent argument broke out. The Armadillo jumped to his feet and started shouting at Eduardito.

Rosalinda returned to where we were sitting. 'Eduardito is our ally,' she said, ignoring Dot's protests. 'To hurt or kill him now would ruin our chances.'

'She's right,' I said to Dot. 'What The Armadillo really said was that he wants to tie us to your truck tyres and set them on fire.'

Dot gasped.

'Do you think your father will agree to come here?' I asked Rosalinda.

'He told me he wants people of all political persuasions to join his new administration,' she answered while listening to the argument. 'It's the only way he can get Peru working again.'

'Even the Shining Path?'

'Everybody.'

'This whole thing could be a trap. What's to prevent Eduardito from killing your father if he comes here?'

'Terrorists aren't used to working with other people,' Dot said. 'Look at Fidel Castro. He shot everyone who disagreed with him.'

The dispute between Eduardito and The Armadillo was growing louder. Their voices sounded like the snarling of animals. The others stood by, gripping their guns, looking tense and worried.

'What are they saying?' Dot asked.

'Eduardito has told him what he's going to do, and The Armadillo has called him a coward and a traitor.'

'Uh oh. Those are fighting words.'

The words were hardly out of Dot's mouth when The Armadillo grabbed Eduardito by the collar and tried to butt him in the face. Eduardito, being the stronger of the two, pushed him away and hobbled backwards a few steps. The Armadillo, his expression twisted in hatred, advanced on him again. He stopped when Eduardito drew his pistol and pointed it at his belly.

There was dead silence in the room as the two rivals, stiff with anger, attempted to stare each other down.

Arching his back, The Armadillo spat a mouthful of half-chewed popcorn into Eduardito's face.

The lobby lurched with the explosion from Eduardito's gun. There was a burst of smoke and a blaze like lightning that lit up The Armadillo's sneering, dying face. He was simultaneously driven backwards by the force of the slug and bent double like a man who has been punched in the solar plexus. He pitched forward and crashed to the floor. From somewhere inside his body issued a prolonged whimpering or mewing noise. His hands and shoes drummed on the floorboards, raising little plumes of dust. Near the small of his back was a bloody crater you could have sunk your fist into. The whitewashed wall where he had stood was spattered with a crimson rainbow of meat and guts.

'Oh, my God,' Dot whispered.

19

Outside, the wind had dropped. The stars were out – millions of them. Meteors showered down, like some sort of divine, cosmic rain that had been released from the heavens to cleanse the earth of yet another brutal, man-made cruelty.

Using their kalashnikovs as cattle prods, Eduardito's men pushed and poked us along. The truck seemed more sinister than before because our nerves were shattered by the killing and because we knew it had that big gun inside. Eduardito climbed into the cab and got the motor going while the others, who looked as scared as we were, pointed their guns at us and made us keep our hands up. After a while we heard static and whistling noises as he tried to make contact with the outside world. He motioned for Rosalinda to climb up. She began to talk with the radio operator at the military base in Juliaca. The terrorists poked Dot and me with their guns and made us stand back.

'This is Rosalinda Calderón. . . .' Her voice quavered with shock and fright. 'That's right – the President's daughter. I need to speak with my father. . . . That's it – right now. He's at his farm on Juanpablo. There's a brand new telephone so it *must work*. Can you please put me through?'

There was a long series of sporadic and confusing exchanges. Finally she was connected to a general whom she happened to know and who recognized her voice.

'Please put me through to Daddy. . . . No, I'm all right. No, I'm not in any trouble. I just need to talk to him right away.'

After several more minutes of static and delays, the voice of Uncle Joshua came through on a phone patch.

'Yes, Daddy, it's me. . . . Yes, I'm all right. Can you hear me? I can hear you. . . . No, there's nothing wrong. I'm at

Lagunas Lagunillas. . . . That's right, where Charlie used to go fishing. . . . James is with me, yes. . . . I'm sorry, Daddy. I didn't mean to scare you. . . . You got my note, didn't you? . . . Good . . . yes. . . . Tell Mother I'm . . . I know she is. Tell her not to worry, and that James is here and we're both all right. . . . All right. I want to come home now, Daddy . . . I want to go to Lima with you . . . yes, I do. I really do. No, I mean it. Can you come and get me. . . . What? I can't hear you very well now. What? Can you . . . what? Oh, that's better. Tell the pilot he can land. . . . You can land it right here on the soccer pitch. It's flat. You can't miss it, it's right here in front of the hotel. Are the children all there? . . . Good. Are they all right? . . . Good. Daddy, tell them there's an elephant here. . . . An elephant. . . . That's right, a real live circus elephant. . . . No, I'm not joking. It belonged to. . . . What? I said it belonged to that circus Charlie took the children to, the one without an elephant. . . . It was too big for the train to pull over the mountains, so it's been living here all this time in a circus tent. . . . What? Yes. Ha ha. That's right. We all need to be rescued, even the elephant. . . . Yes, I love you, too. What? Hello? I can't hear you . . . your voice is fading. Hello? Daddy? Are you there? Hello! Hello! Hello!'

Eduardito turned off the engine, and the radio went dead.

'Big storm up in Sierra,' he said.

'He'll be here first thing in the morning.' Rosalinda climbed down from the truck. 'He loves his new helicopter and he's going to come here straight from Juanpablo.'

'You forgot the most important thing!' Dot hissed. 'You forgot to tell him Eduardito is here!'

'How could I have? He had a gun pointed at my head. He said General Testino was listening in and if I mentioned his name, he would send soldiers to arrest or kill him before he could give himself up to Daddy.'

'Rosalinda, it's *absolutely vital* that your father should know about this before he comes here.'

'I agree with Dot,' I said. 'I think you should try to contact him again.'

'Big storm in Sierra,' Eduardito repeated. 'Not possible.'

'Listen, you . . . you . . . *killer*,' Dot snapped. 'Make that radio work again right now. If you can't, I will. This place will be crawling with soldiers in the morning. When they see you, they'll shoot first and ask questions later, unless Mr Calderón can tell them to hold off. Your hide won't be worth two cents unless this girl can get through to her father. I think you deliberately cut her off. Now if you want to save your own skin, get back up there and make that thing work!'

To my amazement, Eduardito backed down before the ferocity of Dot's words. He climbed into the truck and tried again, or pretended to. The speaker rattled with static. He couldn't get through.

'You go back to hotel,' he commanded, waving his pistol at us.

'I guess I was lucky to talk to Daddy at all,' Rosalinda said when we were out of earshot.

Lucky or horribly, tragically unlucky, I thought. What if Eduardito were preparing a trap for Uncle Joshua?

Dot wasn't convinced either. 'Now your father is going to walk in here under the illusion that you're perfectly all right, watching elephants and playing soccer. Which is not the case at all, because we're all in the hands of this criminal.'

'I'm sorry. . . . I didn't know what to say.' Rosalinda stumbled. I put my arm around her waist. She was shaking all over. 'I wanted to say something . . . normal.'

'That was the wrong instinct, dearie – the mistaken impulse,' Dot scolded gently.

'How could I have done anything else with a gun pointed at my head?'

'You were in a tight spot,' I agreed. 'But Dot's right – there's no telling what Eduardito might do now.'

'I know he's going to give himself up.'

'How can you be sure he won't change his mind?' I asked.

'He just killed that man – the one who didn't want him to. Isn't that proof enough?'

'Rosalinda, do you know what I think? I think Eduardito deliberately killed The Armadillo to impress you. He didn't have to shoot him . . . he could have knocked him down or tied him up, or taken him outside to tell him in private what his real intention is. I bet he deliberately gunned down The Armadillo in front of our eyes to make you think that he was determined to give himself up, and wouldn't tolerate any opposition. It just goes to show how cunning and ruthless he is. Now he's achieved his aim because by killing The Armadillo he convinced you of his sincerity and got you to call your father.'

'What do you think his real intention is?'

'To lure your father here and kill him.'

Rosalinda gasped. 'I don't believe that.'

'He's killed once and he'll kill again. He's not the old friend you once had, Rosalinda.'

'I know him too well. Eduardito is an idealist.'

'So are a lot of terrorists all over the world. Like Teo said, they talk about paradise on earth while they spray the room with machine-gun fire,' I said. 'I think it's incredible that you still give him the benefit of the doubt.'

'Listen, he was Strongest's best player not just because he had the most talent. He was the most dedicated. He trained the hardest, thought most about the game, and never stopped practising. He was one of the best players in Arequipa. They'd picked him for the national team before he broke his leg. He was a good student, too, even though his family came from the *barriadas*, and he went to the university to study pharmacology. He told me that while he was there he realized he was being trained to fill a niche in the bureaucracy that was the cause of all the injustices he saw around him. But he still hoped he could do some good by opening a pharmacy somewhere in the Sierra where medicines aren't available. He came to Puno Province with the best intentions, and joined an Indian commune.'

'He's conned you,' I said. 'And so how did the idealist get to be a terrorist?'

'Dr Morales changed his life. He said that sincerely.'

'The Shining Path are sincere, too. Don't you see how sincerity can lead to fanaticism?'

'Dearie, you're the one who's talking like an idealist,' Dot said to Rosalinda. 'I just hope your father isn't, too. I hope you didn't learn it from him.'

'I learned everything from him!' Rosalinda, her face streaked with tears, said defiantly.

'Well, if he is, he won't last long as President of Peru,' Dot said. 'He won't last long, period. Thank goodness the President of this country never goes anywhere without soldiers. I hope he arrives here tomorrow with a battalion.'

'Well, he's not President yet – only President-elect. Daddy doesn't like soldiers.'

'If he doesn't bring them, then God help him, because Eduardito will kill him,' I said. 'He never will be President. But if he does bring them, then God help us, because Eduardito will kill us before he gets shot by the soldiers.'

We went inside the hotel. The Armadillo's body still lay on the floor. Melanio and the other Indians had reappeared from wherever they had been hiding. They were standing around looking at it. Blood had soaked through the dirty raincoat and had spread in a puddle around the corpse. Dot was right – a dead man doesn't look like a man any more. The Armadillo's face seemed shrunken, as if the flesh had caved in on the space left by the departed spirit. The body looked smaller with the life gone out of it, and totally, hopelessly, dead. Dot knelt down and frisked him. She pulled a pistol from his pocket, and quickly put it in hers.

20

The hotel generator was shutting down. Melanio handed me a lantern. His face was a mask. It didn't let on what he felt or which side he was on, but I knew instinctively what his expressionless face meant: like the *marutopi*'s game of playing dead, it meant that he wanted to get out of this one alive.

We went upstairs.

For reasons of security, Dot, Rosalinda and I decided to sleep in the same room. The door to Charlie's suite wouldn't lock so we pushed a huge, hand-made mahogany chest of drawers against it. We sat there in the gloom, listening to thumps and bumps above our heads.

'What's going on?'

'Everyone's moving furniture tonight.'

Dot shone her flashlight at the ceiling. 'Everyone's moving because everyone's scared.'

'I thought we were the only people in the hotel,' Rosalinda said.

'Some Indians have probably crept in from their camp.'

'What do they have to be scared of?'

'Johnny said that ever since the Shining Path came into being, locking or blocking doors has become a habit in Peru. Let's see if we can get some sleep.'

'James, while we were walking, Eduardito mentioned some crimes committed at El Gordo and Huanta. Do you know what he was talking about?'

'No,' I lied.

'El Gordo was that mining disaster at Cerro de Pasco,' Dot answered. 'It happened when Thad was working there. Hundreds of Indian miners lost their lives when the Gordo shaft collapsed in an earthquake.'

'The way Eduardito talked about it made me feel guilty, as though he thought that I had something to do with it.'

'The circumstances were kind of suspicious,' Dot explained. 'There had been a strike, the army had been called in, and the pit was surrounded by soldiers. When the disaster happened, Thad and the other American engineers naturally wanted to go down to assess the damage and get the miners out. They were the only ones qualified to do so. But the soldiers stopped them. No one was allowed in. The army said that *they* would handle it. Instead, all the American engineers and their families were put on the train to Lima. They said the Government was giving us an all-expenses-paid holiday. It didn't make any sense, sending the experts away at the moment they were most needed, but we didn't have any choice in the matter. We boarded the train practically at gunpoint.'

I looked at Rosalinda. She was listening intently.

'When we got back,' Dot went on, 'we were told that El Gordo, the richest copper mine in Peru, had been closed for good. The seismograph records had been destroyed. Thad and the others doubted that a tremor had smashed the mine, and we heard rumours that it was dynamite, planted by the soldiers, that had buried the striking miners.'

'When did this happen?' Rosalinda asked. 'How many years ago?'

'Back in the days when your grandfather was President. It was during his first term of office.'

'Did Charlie have anything to do with it?'

'Well, one of the rumours that went around was that he ordered the mine blown up.'

'He would never do such a barbaric thing!' Rosalinda protested fiercely. 'Would he?' she turned to me.

'There were Communists involved,' I said.

'I'll have to ask Daddy if it's true or not. He'll know.'

'Let's get some shuteye,' I said, trying to change the subject. 'It's late.'

'How can you expect me to sleep when I've just heard the most terrible news of my life? If the rumour is true, Charlie is responsible for an unforgivable crime. Our family name is stained with blood. How many miners were there?'

'I don't think anyone knows for sure,' Dot said. 'The mine would have to be re-opened, and someone go down there and count the skeletons.'

'And what did he mean by Huanta, Dot? What happened at Huanta?'

'I don't know. I've never heard of Huanta.'

'Let's go to bed,' I said.

'Johnny will be worried.' Dot looked out the window. 'The train was supposed to have arrived by now.'

Rosalinda was preparing to get into bed. Suddenly she screamed. 'Oh my God! Oh! Help!'

We rushed to her bed. Dot ripped back the covers and shone her light. It was the bloody carcass of the snake, coiled in the bottom of the bed.

'Ugh! What's it doing here?'

Rosalinda was a wreck. Dot hugged her. 'It's all right. It can't hurt you.' She led her to the sofa and made her sit down. 'What a dirty trick!'

I re-lit the lantern and picked up the snake by its tail. It was surprisingly heavy. I opened the window and dropped it out. It had left a dirty, bloody stain on the sheets.

'Why did you have to tell them, James?' Rosalinda suddenly turned on me in a fury.

'Tell what? To who?'

'Why did you wait four years before letting the cat out of the bag? Four years of tiptoeing back and forth between the university and our house, and you had to wait until the very last day before leaving Arequipa to tell them. You may have saved your skin but not mine!'

'I didn't tell anyone anything. The Armadillo saw my picture in the newspaper. . . .'

'You said you showed it to him!' Rosalinda shouted hysterically.

'There, there . . .' Dot tried to soothe her. 'It's that dead snake that's upset you.'

'I didn't,' I said again. 'He was looking over my shoulder. Maybe I was a bit careless. I was drunk. If he hadn't seen the picture then, he would have seen it later, or Dr Morales would have . . .'

'But why did you wait until the very last day?'

'It was a coincidence, I swear. If Charlie had died a week later, none of this would have happened.'

'Don't blame this on Charlie, James. Charlie may be to blame for many things, but he's not to blame for the mess we're in. He's dead!'

'Well, I'm not so sure. . . . Maybe Charlie is to blame. . . .'

'What exactly do you mean?'

'If you believe what the students at the university say, the Shining Path has a special grudge against Charlie. . . .'

'I may have been in England too long, but you've been too long with those students at San Agustín. But it doesn't matter whose side you're on, James. Does it? Our side or their side . . .'

'I'm not on their side. . . .'

'Aren't you? Not in your heart of hearts? Daddy doesn't know whose side he's on.' Tears were streaming down Rosalinda's face. 'That's his weakness. That's why he shouldn't be President. Charlie may not have been perfect, but he succeeded because he knew exactly where he stood. Daddy doesn't. I don't blame you if you're not on our side. Why should you be?'

'I'm not on anybody's side,' I admitted.

'Just like Daddy.' Rosalinda was sobbing quietly. Dot was trying to comfort her when we heard a light tapping noise.

Dot put an ear to the door. 'Who is it?' she asked.

'It's me,' a voice replied in English.

'Who's me?'

'It's Eduardito,' Rosalinda whispered.

'Stay out, you murderer,' Dot shouted. 'Go away!'

'I wish . . . speak with you.'

Rosalinda wiped her nose and got to her feet. 'Let him in,' she said softly. 'I've got to keep talking to him. It's our only chance!'

'Let the murderer say what he has to say through the door,' Dot said.

'James . . .' Rosalinda appealed to me. 'Open the door.'

I shoved the chest aside. The door opened, and Eduardito limped into the room.

Even his limp was graceful; he moved like a wounded animal. 'I sorry . . . for snake,' he said in broken English. 'I know nothing. When I hear you scream, others tell me Pedro do it . . . his joke.'

He was unarmed.

'A dead man's joke,' Dot muttered. Her arms were folded across her chest. The hand holding The Armadillo's revolver was hidden in her armpit.

Watching Eduardito, I felt a kind of admiration swell within me. Those primitive Indian features, so incomprehensible to an outsider, had a kind of ageless grace you don't find in white faces. It was a face that belonged to the earth which, one day, he might inherit. White people, by comparison, with their pale skin and yellow hair, look like invaders from outer space. His beardless cheeks and shock of straight black hair could have belonged to a boy. He was a little older than Rosalinda – about nineteen or twenty years old.

'Two weeks ago . . . in commune of Huarocondo . . . near Cuzco,' he began, glancing at Dot, 'arrive strange box. Big box on wheels. The people of commune . . . very happy to see such big box. They were very hungry . . . they think box have food inside. They come running and stand around . . . wait for food. The American who drive box tell me he come back to Peru after many years. He born here. He say he. . . .' He touched his chest. 'He . . . love . . . Peruvian flag. Something happen to him in Peru. "Peru do funny things to people", he told me. "Things you not forget. Peru change your life".'

Dot let out a little gasp. 'That's Johnny he's talking about!'

'*¿Quien sabe?*' Eduardito reverted to Spanish. 'Our country has, *sin duda*, as great a charm for outsiders as it has detachment from the wide world. The humility of the native Peruvian, his innocence, the ingenuousness or credulousness, comes from being eternally poor and downtrodden by the elements, not to speak of his fellow man. In spite of the crimes committed at El Gordo and Huanta . . .' he went on, staring at Rosalinda, 'he has preserved his *naïveté*, which is the result of his isolation. This does make, I suppose, for great charm, despite the poverty. I think what the man from the United States was driving at was humanity. The humanity of our country – seen everywhere, even in the rocks, he told me – is touching. *Sin duda*. He said he wept when he saw our flag again. . . . He fell to his knees and wept.'

'What's he saying?' Dot asked, perplexed. But Eduardito continued talking.

'He said he was made aware of the power of people without pretence, without much hope, shaped by the struggle yet somehow light-hearted, tough and cheerful. (A fine combination – *¿sin duda?*) He said that Peruvians lacked all trace of arrogance. We had learned that lesson a long time ago, I replied. It wasn't the Spanish who taught us, but the harshness of land and sky, which left us no time for arrogance. Pride I think we take in our own durability. He told me that if the Indian populations were aware of their numbers they would rise up and occupy Lima and La Paz. I doubted this. We are aware of our numbers, I told him, but we didn't see ourselves winning *under any circumstances* in the short term.'

'Is he talking about Johnny?'

'All this time . . . the people of Huarocondo, waiting and waiting,' he spoke again in halting English. 'They very hungry, and they want food in box. The man . . . he open the door to box, and the people see inside not food but books. Many, many books. The man like his books. . . . He start giving them to the people. He tell them best thing in world is to read and write. The mothers . . . who hold up their babies for milk, become angry. Very angry. They start pulling books from box . . . thinking food hidden inside. The American . . . he try to stop them, but too many people . . . too many hungry people. Someone throw stone. It hit the man in face. Blood come out. The people pull all books out of the box, but no food. Only books – many, many books. The women start to throw stones. Many stones. The American fall to knees, just

like he see Peruvian flag. He beg . . . he say no, please stop
. . . but too many angry people with stones. They hit his face
and head. He lie on ground and not move again. The books
. . . the box . . . all burn, burn.'

The revolver discharged close to my head with a deafening
bang. When I opened my eyes, Eduardito had disappeared
through the doorway.

'They killed him! They killed Johnny!' Dot screamed and,
sobbing hysterically, collapsed on to a chair. 'Oh, no! No! No!
They killed my boy!'

Far away in the night, the volcano defiantly spat out sparks
at the sky.

21

At first light Rosalinda put her head out the window. 'They're gone,' she whispered. Her face was deathly pale. There were dark rings under her eyes. She looked haggard.

'How do you know?' I asked.

'The truck is gone.'

'But does that mean they've gone?'

'I don't know, but the truck is nowhere in sight.' She looked down at Dot, who lay asleep on the bed. Rosalinda had been up the whole night talking to her, listening to her cry, and doing everything she could to comfort her. She had finally fallen asleep about an hour ago.

'Eduardito was supposed to give himself up. He swore he would do it.'

'You ought to count your lucky stars he's gone. He's a murderer.'

'He didn't throw the stones at Dot's son.'

'He didn't stop them, either.'

'It sounded like a mob out of control.'

'If he's gone from here, so much the better. The thought of all those soldiers coming must have scared him off,' I said. 'I'm surprised they're not here already.'

'Let her sleep,' Rosalinda said, pulling the covers up to Dot's chin. 'She needs it. She's going to wake up and remember that her son is dead.'

We made our way downstairs. Rosalinda was very unsteady; she leaned on me for support.

'Look!' I said. 'Look at the blood on these stairs!'

'Oh no! Dot must have wounded him.'

'Not just wounded. She must have hit an artery. Look, there's blood spattered everywhere!'

The Armadillo's body had been taken away. No trace of the crime remained. We noticed that the floorboards were a bit paler where they had been scrubbed. The popcorn had been swept up. The gore had been wiped off the wall. It almost seemed like a bad dream that had never really happened.

The row of grinning skulls was a sardonic reminder that murders had been committed. The scene of the crime had been sanitized, yet no one seemed to be around. We wandered through the hotel, shouting, 'Melanio! Melanio!' No one answered.

In the dining room we found that breakfast had been prepared. Three places had been laid, and there were three plates of fresh papaya slices with chunks of lime. The coffee was hot, and in salvers we found fried eggs, fried bananas, and rice.

'*Huevos cubanos*,' Rosalinda said.

'Do you want some?' I asked.

'I'm not hungry.'

'Our last breakfast,' I said.

'Why do you say that? Are we doomed?'

'I mean our last breakfast together before we part company.'

I helped myself. Rosalinda sipped some coffee; then she began to eat. Having been up the whole night with Dot, we were starving.

All the colour had drained from Rosalinda's face. 'What'll we do now?' she asked. She looked sick.

'You must go back with your father to Arequipa. It's too dangerous in Puno Province for you to spend another minute here.'

'You're right, but what about you?'

'I'll go on the train with Dot. Someone has to go with her. We'll report her son's murder in Juliaca. Will you wire my parents in Santa Cruz and tell them what I'm doing? Otherwise they'll be worried when I don't show up.'

'Of course I will,' Rosalinda whispered.

'If necessary I'll accompany Dot to Cuzco and go with her to this Huarocondo to find the body. She'll have to identify it, and she'll need somebody with her to do it. I'll stay with her until Johnny's buried. Then I'll put her on the plane to Lima. Maybe you can meet her there. . . .'

'Yes, you must go with Dot,' Rosalinda said. 'And I must go back and find out the truth about El Gordo. Holding Dot's hand last night, I was trying to put two and two together and reached some . . . horrible conclusions. Right now there's a lump in my throat and a pain inside my head like a hangover going back years and years. I remember El Gordo now. I was only a child at the time, but I remember hearing about it on the radio. And now I think I understand why Charlie didn't serve three consecutive terms in office. I bet that's why he put up his vice-president, old Manzarares, for the intervening term – hoping things would cool off and people would forget. And it may explain why he turned down that offer to write his life story. He didn't want to dredge up the past and face the truth. He was content to take me fishing . . . and to let those memories fade. But there must be people out there, James – hundreds of them, maybe thousands, the miners' families and loved ones – who will never forget and never forgive until justice is done. They must want revenge like those starving Indians craved food. They're waiting for someone to pay the full price for the crimes committed at El Gordo.'

Eustaquio, the boy from the train, came running into the dining room looking worried. 'The train is ready to leave,' he said breathlessly. 'Where's the señora?'

'I'll fetch her,' Rosalinda said, getting to her feet.

A few minutes later she led Dot down the stairs. Dot's eyes stared straight ahead with a fixed, unseeing expression. She was in a state of shock.

'Would you like some coffee?' I asked.

She mechanically swung her head from side to side.

'Eduardito has gone,' I said. 'His truck is gone. You hit him, Dot. You wounded him badly. He may be dead.'

'We're all murderers,' she whispered.

'The train is going to leave,' Eustaquio repeated. His face wore a dark, preoccupied frown.

'Will you walk her down to the train, Eustaquio?' Rosalinda asked. 'I'm going to get some food out of the kitchen. Will you help me, James?'

I followed Rosalinda into the kitchen and watched while she filled a cardboard box with coffee, a bag of sugar, a stack of tortillas, two papayas and four eggs. She fumbled with the eggs, and one fell to the floor and broke.

'She may not be hungry now, but she will be later,' she said, stooping down to clean up the mess. 'She'll need food to keep her strength up for the ordeal that's ahead of her.'

My mind was racing ahead. The change in our fortunes seemed almost too good to be true. Eduardito, wounded and perhaps bleeding to death, had vanished back into the wastes of Puno Province where he had come from. His companions were probably suffering from the effects of rat poison. I could have hugged Rosalinda. I could have cried with joy, had I not known that her heart was going to be broken when she heard the full details of the murders at Cerro de Pasco and Huanta. I felt like a shipwrecked sailor who has crawled out of a shark-infested sea into a leaking lifeboat. The danger was still there, all around us, but not quite as close as it had been before.

'Do you have some money, James?'

'What for?'

'I think we ought to leave something for this food.'

I put some money on the counter. Rosalinda handed me the box and gently took my arm, as though I were an invalid, when she was the one who could hardly stand. Her tired and worn face gave me a glimpse of what she would look like when she was an old woman. 'I'll walk to the train with you,' she said in a barely audible voice.

We went down through the dust. As we passed the tent, the elephant keeper came rushing out.

'There's a truck in here,' he said angrily, 'and Nuria doesn't like the smell.' He shook his fist at Rosalinda. 'The Cork busted our circus!'

We went into the tent, and looked at the truck.

'So he's going to give himself up after all.' The sight of the truck seemed to lift Rosalinda's spirits. 'I wonder where he is.'

'He must be badly wounded. I don't think he could have gone very far.'

'James, do you remember the noise we heard last night? It just occurred to me – that was the same noise my old truck tyre used to make when I rolled it around in my room.'

'Dot is the only one I know who has spare truck tyres,' I said. 'Eustaquio was supposed to be keeping an eye on them, but I thought he looked awfully worried.'

'Maybe they've been stolen and he didn't have the nerve to tell her.'

'I don't think she's interested in those tyres any more.'

'That still doesn't explain why tyres were being rolled around on the top floor of the hotel last night.'

We hurried on to the train.

'It's The Cork's fault the circus never came back!' the keeper called after us. 'Remember El Gordo! Remember the massacre at Huanta!'

'Massacre,' Rosalinda said. 'Everybody knows about these tragedies but me. What a fool's paradise I've been living in!'

The tracks had been repaired. The ancient engine was puffing away, ready to be off again. The Indians were hanging out the windows waving at us to get on board.

Rosalinda hugged me and looked at me with tears in her eyes. 'Goodbye, cousin. I'll never forget this adventure as long as I live. It's made me sadder, older and wiser. I apologize for shouting at you last night. I didn't mean any of it. I take it all back.'

'None of us were in our right minds. We were all scared out of our wits.'

'You were right all along – my place is beside Daddy. He and I have a lot to talk about. After all, if Charlie was responsible for El Gordo, what else was he capable of? I've got to find out what happened at Huanta.'

'I don't like leaving you here by yourself. Eduardito could still be lurking around somewhere.'

'Don't worry. Daddy will be here any minute. I'll be at Juanpablo in an hour.'

I climbed aboard the train and sat down beside Dot. 'Rosalinda packed some food for you,' I said.

'Eustaquio is bringing my tyres from the baggage room,' she mumbled.

The train began to move. Rosalinda was walking alongside.

'I'm so sorry about your son,' she said to Dot.

'My life is over now. I'm not a mother any more, or a wife. Those roles have been taken from me. I'm empty. I don't have any strength left.'

'I wish there was something I could do to help you, but I must go home now.'

'Is there anyone who can tell me where his body is?' Dot asked, distraught. 'Is it under the ground, or hidden under rocks in a shallow grave? Or has it been pushed into a ditch like a dead dog, for the vultures to pick over?' She went on, 'I spent my whole life praying for him. When he was a little boy, I prayed for his health and happiness. Watching him sleep, I prayed to God to keep him safe and strong. When he was away at war, I went to church every day and prayed for his safe return.' Dot was crying again. 'He came home, and I thought the danger was over. . . .'

'James is going to go with you as far as Cuzco. He'll tell the police what happened,' Rosalinda said softly.

'I'm not going to bury him here. I'm going to take his body back to America, I don't care how much it costs.'

'Whatever you decide, James will help you. When it's all over, I hope you'll come and stay with me in Lima.'

Dot looked down at her from the moving train. 'I'm going to give my son a decent burial in America.'

Just then we heard the noise of a helicopter. I craned my neck out the window. I couldn't see it, but the noise was everywhere. It was somewhere on the other side of the train.

Rosalinda saw it first. 'He's here!' she called. 'Goodbye, Dot! Goodbye, James!' She started walking back towards the hotel.

147

Then it came into sight, a tin bird with skis for feet, still some distance away and circling. It was painted red and white – the colours of Peru.

The Indians were excited. They leaned out of the moving train. The words '*El Presidente!*' passed among them as they strained to get a glimpse of the great man who was going to put an end to violence and lead their country into an era of democratic prosperity.

Rosalinda was walking towards the soccer pitch and waving. When the helicopter saw her, it started to descend. She had to retreat to get out of its way.

Head bowed, Eustaquio was standing behind us.

One look at his face told me that something was wrong.

'Where are my Firestones?' Dot asked.

'Gone, mum. Stolen.'

'What did he say?'

'He said they aren't there any more. Someone took them.'

Eustaquio just stood there and gulped.

'Does it matter any more?' I put my hand on Dot's sleeve. 'Do you still want them? Who stole them, Eustaquio?' I asked.

He was silent.

'Eduardito probably took them,' I said to Dot.

'You said he was dead!'

'His truck is in the elephant's tent. He may still be around here somewhere. He's bleeding a lot.'

'Did you see the truck in the tent?'

'Yes.'

'Are my tyres in it?'

'I didn't see them.'

'Is the machine gun still there?'

'No,' I said. 'That's not there, either. Everything has been taken out, even the radio.'

For one long, terrible moment Dot fixed me with a penetrating gaze. Her tear-streaked face, which a minute before had borne an exhausted expression of grief and shock, twitched convulsively as it came back to life. Her eyebrows locked into a deep scowl as she seemed to peer straight into my soul.

'You knew the machine gun had been moved, and you didn't say anything! That means he's going to use it. And you let her stay here!' Open-mouthed, she whirled towards the windows. 'Rosalinda!' she bellowed. 'Oh my God! Rosalinda!'

But Rosalinda couldn't hear. The helicopter was hovering above the soccer pitch, making a terrific racket. The wash from the rotors had created a dust storm, almost obliterating the hotel from view.

Just then I noticed something different about the hotel; it had a new feature which I did not immediately recognize. Then I realized what it was. The window above Charlie's suite was covered by a green tarpaulin like the one that had been thrown over the machine gun in the back of Eduardito's truck.

'Rosalinda!'

The helicopter settled and came to rest. The motor was shut off. The rotors went on swinging for a few seconds as the door opened.

The train was still crawling at a snail's pace. There was a movement next to me. Dot had left her seat and had jumped from the train. She landed on her feet and started running towards the hotel. The pistol was in her hand. She went towards the tent just as the elephant and the keeper came out to see what the fuss was all about.

People started getting out of the helicopter. First came Uncle Joshua, then the children. Rosalinda's brothers and sisters were in the helicopter, too. I could see them – Bayardo, Rosie, Elena, Paul, Clarita and Betsy, the youngest.

Dot was still running along the path that led to the hotel, but no one was paying any attention to her. The children were all looking in the direction of the circus tent.

'Where's the elephant, Daddy?' I could hear them shouting at their father. 'You said there was going to be an elephant!'

They cheered with excitement when the elephant came into view.

Rosalinda joined them. She embraced Uncle Joshua and they stood together, with their arms around each other, surrounded by children, as though they had assembled for a family photograph. The helicopter blades had just stopped turning. The pilot got out, took off his dark glasses and stretched in the morning sun. The dust was settling. Some of the children were vaguely distracted by the sight of the train creeping slowly by, but others were pointing at the elephant, obviously wanting to go over to it. Rosalinda had just noticed Dot, who had charged up on to the edge of the soccer pitch and was running towards her, frantically gesticulating with the pistol. She was pointing towards the hotel, but Rosalinda's back was turned. She did not see the tarpaulin being pulled away from the window above Charlie's suite.

I froze. Like the *marutopi*, I stopped breathing.

Dot's warning came too late because a terrible noise had erupted, an ugly snarling growl that would reverberate to every corner of the country and call down the long night of barbarism upon Peru.

Eduardito was firing the machine gun from the window above Charlie's suite. It was sitting on Dot's truck tyres. One of the terrorists was holding it down, but he could not control the gun. It was jumping all over the place. The bullets were pounding into the soccer pitch, sending up geysers of dust but missing the helicopter completely.

As soon as the shooting started, there was panic. Uncle Joshua was trying to push his children back into the helicopter. He was picking up the littlest ones and throwing them in. The blades began to turn – agonizingly slowly. The machine gun was firing in bursts now, and not so wildly. Eduardito's companions were managing to hold the thing down. Each burst kicked up sprays of dust closer to the helicopter.

Finally the door was shut, Uncle Joshua and Rosalinda being the last to climb aboard. The rotors picked up speed.

I couldn't see the helicopter any longer. It was lost in the dust storm blown up by the rotors. My heart was in my throat. The dust was going to save them. The gun stopped firing. Maybe it had jammed, or maybe Eduardito had used up all the ammo. Maybe he had fainted from loss of blood. Slowly the helicopter rose from the cloud of dust and came into view. I could see faces at the window. Hundreds of Indians were hanging out the slowly moving train watching the drama in dead silence. Then we heard the gun fire again.

But the helicopter was airborne; it was going to get away. There was a long, final burst, followed by a moan from the Indians. The helicopter shuddered and stopped rising. Bits of metal were flying off it. A rotor snapped and went cartwheeling through the air. The helicopter tipped forward and fell back to earth where Dot stood with her arms outstretched as if to catch it. It landed in a fiery explosion that did not drown out the screams of the Indians as the little engine puffed away towards the hills.